If It's A Question of my Heart: A Hood Love Story

Leondra LeRae'

Chapter One

Mercedes

I walked through the mall carrying a variety of bags from different stores as I prepared for the holiday season. Between the lightly snow-covered ground and the holiday hustle and bustle, it was beginning to feel a lot like Christmas.

"You good, Cedes?" my sister Alexus asked. Yes, I know. My parents named us after cars. When I was born, they both drove Mercedes Benz. When Lex was born, you guessed it, they both drove a Lexus'. My younger brother came during the peak of my father's career as a surgeon and they named him after dad's most favorite car, Ferrari. I

1

guess, either my mother had enough of having kids since she had her son or she got sick of naming kids after cars because after Rari, she tied her tubes. I was glad too. I had one brother and one sister; I was good.

"Cedes," Lex called again.

"Yeah," I answered snapping out of my thoughts.

"You alright?"

"Yeah, I'm good."

"You think you bought enough gifts?" she laughed. I had to laugh too.

"Yeah, I just gotta get something for Rari Jr."

"Dang, it still seems odd that our little brother has a child," Lex stated.

"Tell me about it, but I love Lil Rari."

"Me too. Let's go to this toy store," she suggested. I followed her into Toys "R" Us and instantly became flustered. Seeing as how Lil Rari is the only really young child in the family, I had no idea what to get him.

"Let me call Rari's mom and see what he likes," I said as I shifted all of my bags to one arm. I didn't miss Lex rolling her eyes. None of us could stand Janayah, but we tolerated her for the sake of our nephew. She gave big Rari enough hell, so we didn't need anymore.

"Hello," she answered.

"Hey. Lex and I are out Christmas shopping. We were wondering what little things Rari likes and if he needs clothes or anything." I had a feeling Janayah was about to be on some bullshit.

"You don't know what your nephew wants or needs? The fuck y'all be doing when he's there?"

I swear, I didn't condone men hitting women but Rari needed to knock this bitch out.

I sighed.

"Janayah, I'm just trying to see if there's anything he needs for your house."

"Oh, so now y'all think I need help taking care of my son?" she snapped.

"That's not what I'm saying. Fuck! Why are you so fuckin' difficult? I'll call his father." I hung up before she could respond. I quickly dialed my brother's number.

"What it do, sis?"

"Could you have knocked up a worse bitch?" I asked.

"What are you talking about?"

I ran down the conversation with Janayah. I heard my brother sigh.

"She's ridiculous. I know she's gonna call me with some bullshit. Just grab him a few outfits if you want. He's a 2T. He likes race cars, tracks, and Tonka trucks." He paused.

"Here she is calling me now. Text me if you need anything else."

"Alright. Thanks, Rari."

We ended the call and I dropped my phone in my bag.

"I swear I want to beat her ass," Lex said as she looked at a Tonka dump truck.

"You and me both."

We continued to shop. I grabbed Rari Jr. a couple of cars with tracks and Lex grabbed him the Tonka trucks. We then headed into True Religion to grab a couple of outfits. My man's birthday was the day after Christmas, so we always celebrated for both days. He always rented out club Encore and balled the fuck out.

My phone rang, breaking me from searching for a shirt. I smiled when I noticed it was Kaseem.

"Hey babe," I answered.

"What's good ma? Where you at?"

"Still at the mall with Lex."

"Damn. Am I gonna be surprised with the credit card bill this month?"

"Nah," I chuckled. "Maybe after Black Friday, you'll be pissed."

He laughed.

"I'm fuckin' with you, boo. I was just calling to see

what you wanted for dinner tonight."

"You know I don't care," I said as I placed two t-shirts, a button-up and two pairs of jeans on the counter.

"Steaks on the grill?"

"Yep."

"A'ight. I'll see you when you get home."

"Okay. Love you."

"Love you more."

I hung up the phone just as the cashier bagged the items.

"Your total is $224.64," she said. I loved True Religions' clearance rack. I always found good shit at a cheap price. I counted out $230 cash and handed it to her. Once we finished, Lex and I said our goodbyes and went our separate ways.

As I climbed in the car, I thought about my relationship with Kaseem. Kas and I have been together for three years. He was my first real relationship. He was technically my first everything. Growing up, I was a homebody. While Lex and Rari hung out with their friends, I was home watching TV. I had little to no friends. I went to school and went home. When I graduated high school, I got a job as a teacher's assistant at the local elementary school and went to school at night. It was my goal to become a second-grade teacher.

It wasn't always easy, but I managed. I met Kas when I was a junior in college. I was nervous when he and I started kicking it. I knew he was probably used to more experienced females and here I was, knowing little to nothing. Surprisingly, he was okay with that and didn't pressure me for anything. Not only did he wait until I was ready for everything, but he treated me like I was a queen and supported me throughout my college career.

I remembered the day we met like it was yesterday. I was sitting in Starbucks studying for midterms. I was grabbing my second coffee when he walked up behind me. His Creed cologne crept up and through my nostrils. I was used to the scent due to it being Ferrari's favorite. I turned around and came face to face with one of the most handsome men I've ever laid eyes on. There he stood about 6'3", chocolate with a full beard along with a head full of hair that was pulled up into a bun. I could tell it was thick yet manageable.

"Here you go," the Starbucks worker stated as she broke me from my trance. I turned back around and grabbed my coffee and rushed off to the table where my belongings were. My virgin like pussy was leaking at the sight of that man. I sat back down and got back to work. It wasn't long before that Creed cologne was back invading

my space. Looking up, pushing my glasses up, I locked eyes with the handsome man again. I squeezed my legs together trying to stop the feeling I was feeling. This was all new to me. I never came across a man who woke my lower region up like he had.

"Can I help you?" I asked trying to mask my nerves. I began playing with the ends of my braids.

"Is anybody sitting here?" he asked pointing to the chair on the opposite side of the table. I shook my head. He sat down with his bottle of water. "What's your name?"

"Mercedes."

He chuckled and I instantly became defensive.

"Something wrong with my name?"

"Not at all. It's funny to me because I always liked the name and said if I had a daughter, I would name her Mercedes."

I blushed and dropped my head.

"Anyway," he continued. "I'm Kaseem, but you can call me Kas."

"Nice to meet you."

We continued talking for another half an hour before we exchanged phone numbers.

That was the start of us. I thanked God every day for that day because Kas has shown me true love since then.

Chapter Two

Kaseem

I hung up the phone with my love and headed inside my boy Jay's crib. Jay and I have been friends since we were eight. He was more like a brother to me. We had each other's backs like no other.

"What's good, Kas?" he greeted me as I walked in.

"Can't call it. What's up with you?"

"Shit just finished counting up bread. You know how that goes."

I did. Jay, myself, his brother Junior and my brother Shaheem owned several businesses from laundry mats to apartment complexes, to car lots and even a couple of gas stations. They're all fronts for our true money-making business. We ran a lucrative drug business as well as gun trafficking. We had a couple of UPS and FedEx workers in our pockets. I had a cousin who was a detective and Jay's older sister was a lawyer.

As you can see, we had our hands in everything. Before you wonder too long, no, Mercedes didn't know about what I really did. She knew I owned the legit businesses but nothing about my illegal activities. Despite us being together for over three years, I wanted to keep my illegals activities from her as long as possible.

"Has there been any BS going on in the streets?" Cedes and I had been on a weekend getaway. To avoid any major suspicions, I kept my phone off when Cedes and I were away.

"Nah. One of the block boys was approached by some new niggas tryna be down."

"Did he say who?"

"Nah."

I shrugged. "Lil nigga must not want to be down that bad. If he does, he'll resurface."

Jay nodded.

"Anyway, how was your getaway?"

"It was cool. We went to Atlantic City. I ain't really a gambler but we enjoyed ourselves."

Just as I finished, Jay had rolled a blunt for us to share. I sat back on the couch and watched him light it.

"When is your bitch ass gonna settle down?" I asked as he passed me the blunt. He began laughing, causing himself to choke.

"When I find a chick who accepts what I do. I respect your relationship with Cedes, but I could never live a double life."

"Nigga, I live one life."

Jay sucked his teeth.

"My nigga, Cedes knows about Kas the businessman, but she has no idea about Kas the hustla."

I couldn't say anything because he was right.

"I'ma tell her."

"You've been saying that for the past three years."

I sucked my teeth.

"The time ain't right," I countered.

"When's it going to be right? First off, I highly double she's gonna leave you. You just gotta tell her before she either finds out from someone else or somehow, God forbid we get knocked," he explained.

Jay made perfect sense.

"A'ight man. Forget I even asked you shit," I chuckled. Jay hated that Cedes knew nothing about what I really did.

I personally felt as if it was best. I mean how would it look that a second-grade teacher was dating one of Rhode Island's top drug dealers? It wasn't a good look and I wasn't trying to publicly ruin her image.

I kicked it at Jay's crib for another hour until my brother Shaheem called, letting me know he was on his way to my house. I dapped Jay up and took off towards the crib.

It took me all of fifteen minutes to get home. I just so happened to pull up at the same time Sha did.

"What's good, nigga?" he greeted when we both got out the car.

"Can't call it. What's good Shanie?" I said to his girl Shandra. Shaheem and Shandra had been together for about a year. I was surprised because usually, Sha switched his women like he switched his draws and trust me, that was a nigga who showered several times a day.

"Hey, Kas. Where's Cedes?" he asked.

"If she ain't inside, she'll be pulling up."

Cedes usually parked her Charger in the garage when she was home for the night. Once I opened the door, I heard music coming from the bedroom.

"She's upstairs. I'll go get her."

That was one thing I never allowed. If it wasn't Cedes or me, nobody went upstairs. The living room, kitchen, and basement, only with me, and the backyard were the only places niggas were allowed when they came to visit.

I jogged upstairs and opened my bedroom door. Cedes had the bathroom door open as she was in the shower. She was singing her ass off to Monica. I stood in the doorway listening to her. My lady could sing. I mean she could give Whitney Houston a run for her money… before her drug days, that is. I could listen to her sing every day.

Five minutes later, she shut the water off still singing.

"Hey," I spoke up so she wouldn't be startled when she opened the curtain.

"Hey, baby. When did you get home?" she questioned as she grabbed her towel.

"Couple minutes. I was listening to you sing."

"You're such a creep," she laughed. I smiled as I stared at her thick frame. Most men loved skinny chicks, but I needed my lady with some meat. Cedes was a solid size sixteen. Her triple D breasts were every bit of perfect to me. I bit my lip as I watched her move around the bathroom. "What are you looking at?"

"My lady. Is there an issue?"

She didn't say anything else. She smiled and shook her head.

"You know I love you, girl," I told her.

"Yeah, yeah I love you too."

"Hurry up though. Sha and his girl are downstairs."

She sucked her teeth and rolled her eyes. Cedes didn't care for Shanie but she tolerated her.

"Be nice."

"I'll be nice when Shaheem gets rid of her gold-digging ass."

I shrugged and shook my head. Cedes was the only one besides Sha who talked to Shanie. She felt like she was using Sha for his money. Sha didn't see it and I wasn't tryna get to know her like that to see if it was true.

"Why do you keep saying that?" I asked. Usually, I didn't ask but I was kind of interested in seeing what she knew.

"I've never met a bitch who had no drive to do anything. Like she bitches if Sha's at work and not answering his phone. She bitches if she doesn't have a certain about of money at her fingers. The shit is annoying."

"If Sha loves it, who are we to kill his vibe?"

"You're his older brother. You should have his best interest."

"I do. He's a grown-ass man though, so he's gonna make his own decisions."

She shook her head yet didn't say anything else. I

truthfully had no idea what she wanted me to do. Shaheem was grown. He did what he wanted and didn't listen to anyone.

I left out the room leaving Mercedes to get dressed. Despite her not caring for Shanie, she would still come downstairs and entertain her for the time they were here. I would just listen to her bitch later.

Chapter Three

Mercedes

I purposely took my time getting dressed. I really didn't fuck with Shanie, but I tolerated her for the sake of Shaheem. I do wish he would open his eyes and see her for the gold-digging hoe she is.

Thirty minutes later, I made my way downstairs.

"It's about time," Kas said. I rolled my eyes and said hi to both Sha and Shanie.

"You have any wine?" Shanie asked. It took everything in me to not say anything smart. Instead, I walked to the kitchen, grabbed a small bottle of wine for Shanie, Henny for Sha and Kas and a bottle of water for me. I grabbed a couple of shot glasses for the guys and headed back towards the living room. I tossed the wine next to Shanie and handed the Henny and glasses to Kas.

"Why are you drinking water?" Kas questioned.

"Because I want water."

He was getting on my nerve already.

"Do you have to be a smart ass?"

I ignored his question.

"Yo," he said. I still ignored him. He stood up and walked over to me. "Let's go."

His stern voice let me know that he wasn't playing. Kas never put his hands on me but I knew when he meant business. I sucked my teeth and followed him upstairs.

"What's your issue?" he questioned the moment I crossed the threshold.

"Nothing at all."

"Try that lie on someone who doesn't know you. The fuck is wrong with you?"

"You started with your smart ass remarks the moment I walked downstairs."

"I know you, Mercedes. You purposely took forever."

"And? I don't like the bitch so why would I rush?"

"You know what? Forget it!"

He walked out of the room leaving me there alone. If I

wasn't hungry, I probably would have stayed in my room.

When I made it back downstairs, I noticed the guys were no longer in the living room. I figured they made their way outside to the back porch so Kas could begin grilling. Shanie sat on the couch watching TV. I went into the kitchen to start peeling potatoes to whip up a potato salad.

"Are you okay, Cedes?" Shanie inquired coming into the kitchen.

"Yup."

"Can I ask you something?"

Hell no, I thought to myself.

"Go ahead."

"What's the secret to you and Kas' relationship?"

"Huh?"

"I mean how do you get Kas to give you access to everything? It's almost like he trusts you with everything."

"He does. I mean, I don't really know what you want to know. I don't ask Kas for anything. I have my own career. There is no secret. We're just us," I shrugged. "Kas is who he is. If he went broke tomorrow, I would still love and want to be with him. I guess the answer is love and be with someone because you love them and want to be with them. Don't be with him because of what he can do for you financially."

"See, I love Sha, but I don't know if I would stick around if he went broke."

"So, you're with him for his money?" I just wanted her to admit she was a gold digger.

"Nah."

"I'm sorry, you're not a gold digger but you won't remain by your man if he fell on hard times. So, what exactly are you?"

"I'm a chick who loves her man but has become accustomed to a certain lifestyle. Regardless, I'm not willing to give it up."

I simply shook my head. Sha's gotta be the dumbest mothafucka not to see beyond this girl's ways.

"So, when y'all go on dates, who pays?" she asked.

"Kas, but I offer all the time."

"You're crazy! Even though you have a career, I would still be banking mine and spending his."

"Well, that's the difference between you and me." I put the potato and peeler down. "I'm a grown-ass woman. I work for mine and spoil my man and while he does the same. I couldn't consider myself a woman if I wasn't bringing shit to the table. My nigga is not my father. It's not his responsibility to take care of me because I want to be lazy. So, if you want a successful relationship, bring something to the table besides pussy."

"You think that's all I have to offer?" I could tell she felt some type of way, but I was sick of biting my tongue.

"Tell me what you have to offer besides some shit every other bitch has to offer?"

"It almost sounds like you're jealous."

"Jealous of what?" I shouted. I was sure Kas and Sha heard me. "Let me check you right quick, Shandra. There ain't a damn thing you got going for yourself that I'm jealous of, sweetie. Ninety percent of the goals I set for myself, checkmark bitch! They've been achieved. My nigga loves the fuck outta me and I love the fuck outta him. The only thing you love is Shaheem's money. The day he opens his fuckin' eyes and sees the shit, will be the saddest day in your fuckin' life."

"What the hell is going on?" Kaseem questioned.

"Your girl is a jealous ass bitch," Shanie stated. I tried charging across the island, but Kas caught me midway.

"What the fuck am I jealous of?" I screamed. "Shandra, you're a fuckin' joke, bro. You have nothing I want. I'm jealous of you yet you're asking me the secret to my relationship. You ain't shit but a gold-digging ass bitch! Tell Sha how you just fuckin' said if he ever fell on hard times, you were dippin! Go ahead. Since you wanna run your fuckin' trap, run your own shit."

I officially had enough of this bitch. Sha stared at her. I felt bad because I could see the hurt in his eyes.

"Really Shanie?" he asked. Kas was still holding me. Livid was mildly explaining how I felt.

"Why are you listening to her?" she inquired with a shaky voice.

"Lie, bitch! I want you to!"

"Shut it," Kas snapped.

"If I went broke tomorrow, Shanie, what would you do? How would you help me?"

"I-I would get a job or something," she stuttered.

I couldn't stop the scoff that escaped from my mouth. Kas cut his eyes at me.

"Hmmm, but as long as I got dough, you won't work? I'll tell you what. You have twenty-four hours to get your shit out my crib."

Thank God, I thought to myself.

"What? Shaheem, are you serious?"

"As a fuckin' heart attack. I'll never go broke, but the last thing I need is a bitch that's using me for my dough."

"I'm not using you."

"I'm not tryna hear that. You heard what I said," he said as he walked away.

"Now carry your lying ass up out my fuckin' house," I spat. I didn't miss the tears dancing in her eyes. I didn't feel bad for her. If anything, I felt bad for Sha. I watched her as she walked out.

"You happy now?" Kaseem asked.

"I'm satisfied, but I won't be happy until I beat her ass."

"Would you chill?" he chuckled. "You finish your potato salad and I'll check on my brother."

Kas kissed my cheek and walked out. I turned Pandora on and finished cutting potatoes. Once I got the pot on, I ran to grab my purse from behind the door and headed to the bathroom. For the past month, I had been feeling off. My breasts were tender, I was always beyond tired and I felt myself being a snappy bitch. I hoped this test would come back positive.

For the past year and a half, Kas and I had been actively trying to conceive. We've suffered three miscarriages in the past and every day I prayed for my miracle, rainbow baby. Every time I found out that I was pregnant, I would go to my first ultrasound and they wouldn't find a heartbeat. I was crushed every time I walked out of the doctor's office.

I pulled my pants down, removed the stick from the package, and peed on it. Once I was done, I sat the test on the sink and took a deep breath. Between the miscarriages and the negative pregnancy tests, I was on the verge of giving up. I kept a small piece of hope that my miracle would come. I stared in the mirror and gave myself a pep talk.

"Despite what this test reads, you're still worthy. You're still amazing. You're still Kaseem's dream woman. The both of you will get through anything that is thrown your way. Put all your fears in God's hands."

I smiled at myself as I flipped the test over and took another deep breath.

Pregnant 3+ sat on the screen. There is was. According to this digital test, I was more than three weeks pregnant. I could not stop the smile that spread across my face. *Thank you, God,* I thought to myself. I contemplated on when I wanted to tell Kas. Thanksgiving was about two weeks away. I wanted to tell him before then but then a part of me wanted to wait until I had an ultrasound to say anything. I knew I couldn't keep it from him that long.

I washed my hands, dropped the test back in my purse and headed out to the kitchen to finish the potato salad.

God, I know you've been hearing from me a lot lately, but I want nothing more than to carry this baby to term and deliver a very happy and healthy baby. Kaseem and I want this so bad. Please allow us to enjoy not only this pregnancy but our child as well! Amen!

Chapter Four

Kaseem

I sat at the grill flipping the steaks as I watched Shaheem throwback shots.

"Be easy, Sha," I said.

He shook his head.

"I shoulda known, man. She showed many signs of being a gold-digging ass bitch. I just tried to overlook them, hoping it was just my mind fuckin' with me. I'm just glad sis called it out before shit got any deeper," he said taking another shot.

"She has been saying it for a while now. I just told her to mind her business."

"I wish she woulda told me."

I started feeling bad now.

"It'll be alright, bro," I assured him.

"Nah, I know. We just worked too hard to build what we got to let any bitch knock us off. No worries. My bounce back is about to be real."

I dapped my brother up as we continued to chop it up. Sha and I were our parents' only two children. We were two years apart, but he truly was my best friend. We got into both our legal and illegal business together. I didn't want him in the drug game, but he was adamant. I knew if I didn't work with him, he would find someone else who would. I tried keeping him more involved in our legal businesses to keep his nose as clean as possible.

"I needed a new bitch anyway. Someone with more motivation. Someone like Cedes who grinds for her own," he said.

I smiled.

"Cedes is one of a kind. I thank God for her for real."

Twenty minutes later, Cedes came out.

"What's up, babe?"

She didn't say anything but wore a Kool-Aid smile. She tossed something in my direction. I grabbed it and realized it was a pregnancy test. I glanced at her before looking at the window.

"This is real?" She nodded her head rapidly. "Wow!" I walked over to her, picked her up and spun her around.

"I'm praying this is the one," she said with tears in her eyes.

"This is it," I assured her. I planted kisses all over her face.

"Shit, can I get in on the excitement?" Sha asked.

"God willing, we'll be parents," I told him.

"Congrats man! I know what y'all have been going through. I'll definitely keep y'all in prayers."

"Nigga, you don't pray," I joked.

"Shut your bitch ass up," Sha replied.

For the rest of the night, we laughed, ate and talked shit to each other. I couldn't have asked for a better night.

*****

The following day was Sunday. Sundays were the days that Cedes and I relaxed. We very rarely left the house. We kicked back and watched TV for most of the day and got housework done. When I was in my young and dumb days, nobody could ever tell me I was spending Sundays in the crib cooking and cleaning with a chick but since being with Cedes, I couldn't picture spending my Sunday's any other way. Mercedes changed me. She made me want more and better out of life. I looked at her and her siblings and I wanted to raise a family like that. Her brother, Ferrari, seemed to be the only one still trying to figure out life. I couldn't judge him though because many didn't get their shit together until their mid-twenties. I offered to give him a job at one of my businesses to keep him out of the streets. I, myself, knew how easy it was to get sucked into the street life and if I could prevent another young brother from being sucked in, I would.

I rolled over and noticed that Cedes was still sleeping. I kissed her cheek and headed to the bathroom to handle my hygiene. I decided to make her breakfast in bed. I pulled out the bread, eggs, milk, bacon, and cinnamon out of their spots. Bacon with French toast and eggs were on the menu.

I threw on my trap music and got busy.

While in the middle of cooking, Cedes appeared rubbing her eyes.

"Good morning, beautiful. I was hoping to have this done before you woke up."

"Smelling this bacon woke me up," she responded as she popped a piece of bacon in her mouth. She then walked over and planted a kiss on my lips. She grabbed another piece of bacon and sat at the table. "What's the plans for today?"

"It's Sunday, ma. We usually stay home," I reminded her.

"Can we switch it up? Maybe a date day or something?"

"A'ight, sounds cool. After breakfast, we'll shower and start our day."

She smiled and jumped out of her seat. Seeing her so excited made me happy. It was the smallest things that made her happy, yet I never minded going all out for her.

I finished making breakfast, made our plates and headed up to the room. Cedes was there flipping through channels. I placed her plate in front of her. I joined her as she settled on the *First 48* reruns.

An hour and a half later, we were hand in hand walking out of the front door. Cedes looked beautiful to me in her jeans, with her riding boots, North Face and Gucci glasses. It was simple but to me, sexy as fuck.

"Okay, where to first?" I asked as we climbed into my navy-blue Range.

"I'm in the mood to shop a little."

"You didn't shop enough yesterday?"

"Christmas shopping for others versus shopping for yourself is two different things."

"Yeah, and I can only imagine the Black Friday dent you're gonna make."

Leondra LeRae'

She laughed and threw her head back.

"I'll probably just get a few electronics. I would rather prepare for our little one," she said. The thought of having a little one on the way made me proud as fuck. I seriously prayed because I couldn't stand to see Cedes hurt behind another miscarriage.

"We can finally put that empty ass room to use."

"Do you want a boy or a girl?" she asked.

"I want a healthy baby," I told her. That was the honest truth too. The gender didn't matter to me. As long as my baby came out healthy, I was fine.

I jumped on 95 North towards Emerald Square Mall. I listened as Cedes sang along with the radio.

"Let me ask you something," I said interrupting her singing.

"Sup?"

"Have you ever wanted to be a singer?"

She shrugged.

"When I was a little girl I did, but now I love my career. I can't see doing anything else."

I nodded but didn't say anything.

Twenty minutes later, I pulled into the mall parking lot. I locked up my truck, grabbed my baby girl's hand and headed inside. I watched as she walked from store to store.

Each time she would try and pay but I never allowed her to spend her money. Even when she did, I would simply call and transfer the money from my account to hers. She talked shit all the time, but I felt as if it was my responsibility to take care of her.

"Babe, let's go to Footlocker," she suggested.

"You go ahead; I'll catch up with you."

I watched her as she took off and I headed to the jewelry spot.

"Can I help you sir?" the worker greeted.

"Give me a minute to look."

"We have this section over here that's on clearance if it's more your budget."

I stopped looking and twisted my face at her.

"Excuse me?"

The bitch had the nerve to repeat herself.

"I think you've lost your fuckin' mind. I probably bring in more in one week than you bring home in a month. I could buy anything in this bitch, and it won't make a dent in my spending limit on my credit card or my bank account. Maybe you need clearance but don't ever fuckin' think I need clearance shit. Where's your supervisor?" This broad had me fuming.

"I'm sorry, sir," she said clearly nervous.

"Fuck your apology. Where's your supervisor?"

Before she could say anything else, an older, well dress woman appeared.

"Is there an issue, Jess?" she questioned the employee.

"Her judgmental ass is the issue," I snapped. "What, because I'm black, you think I'm broke?"

"N-no, sir," Jess replied.

"Okay, what happened?"

"I walked in and this ignorant ass instantly assumed I'm broke and tries to direct me to the fuckin' clearance section. If it's one thing I am, it's far from broke."

"Sir, let me apologize."

"Fuck your apology and fuck this store. I promise that you won't get business from me or anybody I fuck with. Mark my words."

I turned around and walked away before either of them could say anything else.

I met Cedes as she walked out of Footlocker. I'm sure my frustration was plastered on my face.

"Hey, what's wrong?" she asked as she handed me the bag.

"Bitch in the jewelry store just pissed me off. I walked in and the bitch automatically assumed I was broke."

"Oh boy," she said as she shook her head.

"You done?"

"I want something to eat." I couldn't do anything but chuckle. I don't know how I didn't notice her appetite picking up. I didn't say anything as I grabbed her hand and headed to the food court. It didn't matter how pissed I was or who pissed me off, seeing my lady's face and hearing her voice, instantly changed my mood. She truly was the light of my life. She may have thought she was blessed to have me, but it was definitely the other way around. I was blessed to have her.

Chapter Five

Mercedes

I stuffed my face with onion rings from Burger King as Kas sat and stared. There was no shame in my fame. When I was hungry, I ate. I didn't care where I was or who was around. I wasn't about to be shy in front of anybody.

Once I was done, I was ready to go. Kas threw my trash away, as I gathered my bags.

"What the hell did you get from Victoria Secret this time? Don't you think you have enough cheeksters, thongs, demi bras and all that shit?"

I busted out laughing. I didn't know if Kas really studied

my underclothes or if he had just looked at every damn Vicky's receipt I had.

"You can never have too many, especially when they have a panty raid," I said.

"You just look for a reason to buy underwear and shit."

"I buy underwear the like you buy sneakers," I pointed out.

"Oh, don't go there," he laughed. "You buy kicks all the damn time too."

I shut my mouth because he had a valid point. Before I met Kas, I wasn't into shit but flats, Uggs, sandals and sometimes heels. I never met a man who was into having matching kicks with his girl. One thing I could say though was whether I was dressed up or dressed down, Kas loved everything I wore. We made small talk as we walked out of the mall hand-in-hand.

"What do you want to do for Thanksgiving?" I asked him.

"You know my moms usually cooks but I also know you like spending time with your family as well."

"How about we do this, we invite both families over to the house, we'll host Thanksgiving and we can use that time to share the pregnancy announcement with everyone," I beamed.

He smiled.

"I'm with it, as long as we get an ultrasound before then, I'm cool."

I turned my head and didn't let him see my smile drop. I knew why he said it, but I had been so wrapped up in claiming this pregnancy as a successful one that I didn't bother to wonder about that first ultrasound.

"Hey," he called out breaking me from my thoughts. "Be positive, mama. This time will be different."

I gave him a small smile, but I still couldn't help but wonder. I closed my eyes and prayed to God for a safe and healthy pregnancy.

"What do you want for Christmas?" he asked changing the subject and trying to lighten the mood.

"A healthy baby."

"Well, the baby will be too soon to come then."

"That's not what I meant," I laughed. "I meant to be carrying a very healthy baby."

"I know, ma. I know."

We tossed ideas back and forth for Christmas gifts as we headed back home. Once we got home, I stripped down to a pair of shorts and a tank top and started cleaning. Our house wasn't dirty, but it had become a ritual for us to clean on Sundays. Once it was all said and done, I joined

Kas in the living room and watched the Patriots' game. I couldn't understand a lick of football but Kas seemed to like when I watched it with him. I pulled out my phone and started texting Lex.

"Babe," I said during mid-text.

"Wassup?"

"What if we hooked Lex up with Sha?"

Kas pulled his eyes from the TV and stared at me.

"As long as we've been together if they wanted to hook up, I'm sure they would have by now."

"True. But shit, he needs someone new after that shit with Shanie's bitch ass."

"Don't get yourself all worked up behind their BS. If Lex and Sha want to link, by all means, let them, but I'm not about to sit here and play matchmaker."

I chuckled and continued to text my sister. I was also curious as to what happened between Janayah and Rari too.

Me: Hey bro, what happened with you and Nayah yesterday?

As I waited for him to respond, I began browsing Facebook. I came across a post that Shanie had made and couldn't help but shake my head.

Dopegirl Shanie: People love running their mouth about things they know nothing about but let their shit be ran, they start cryin' like a little bitch. It's cool, cuz Shanie knows shit that MF don't think I know. Everything that glitters ain't gold. Watch me work!

I rolled my eyes and continued scrolling until Rari's text came through

Rari: *I got in her ass for being difficult as fuck! Of course, she threatened not to let me see Lil Rari, but I told her to try me if she wants to and I'll drag her ass right up in court and make her life hell. She better stop fuckin' with me*

Me: *LOL, I've never met a chick who makes it hard for a father to be in their child's life. Then again, ratchet BMs do that when they can't be with the father*

I loved my nephew to death, but I wish he had a different mother or that Janayah would just be easier to work with.

Rari: *I'll never be with her again. Hell, I was never with her in the beginning. Drunk nights and slip-ups sometimes result in babies. I love my son though LOL*

I couldn't help but laugh at my simple ass brother.

"What's so funny?" Kas questioned.

I showed him the text and he chuckled too.

"Check this out," I pulled up Shanie's Facebook post and he shook his head but went back to watching TV. I

41

started thinking about my pregnancy. From experience, I knew they could schedule me for an ultrasound for a few weeks out and I really wanted at least one by the time Thanksgiving rolled around. I began googling places that did ultrasounds that I could pay for. I found a couple and screenshot the name, address, and telephone number.

"If I scheduled an appointment for an ultrasound at a place outside of the hospital, would you be able to come?" I asked.

"Babe, I wouldn't care if you scheduled the appointment in Guam for tomorrow at seven in the morning, I'll be there," he said without even taking his eyes off of the TV.

I smiled and leaned in to place a kiss on his cheek.

"I love the hell out of you," I told him.

"I love you too. Now let me finish watching this game so we can cook and get ready for the workweek." I kissed his cheek again then started searching Pinterest for nursery ideas. I could hardly hide my excitement. I had waited so long for this and felt in my heart like it was finally happening for us.

Chapter Six

Kaseem

Once the game was over, I headed into the kitchen to give Cedes a hand.

"What's on the menu tonight, beautiful?" I asked

"I have a taste for chicken parm with a salad."

"Hold the salad for me," I chuckled. I was all for eating healthy, but I wasn't about to eat like a rabbit. I washed my hands and helped out wherever I could. We laughed and talked; it was times like this that I cherished the most. In the business I was in, I could be shot down and killed at any moment if I wasn't careful so I cherished every possible moment I could with my family. As we were sitting at the island discussing random things, my phone began vibrating in my pocket. Pulling it out, I saw it was my mother.

"Wassup, Ma?" I answered.

"Tell Mercedes to go piss on a stick," she said, skipping all the formalities.

"Huh?"

"You heard me! I done dreamt of fish and I already know that your brother isn't knocking up the ditzy broad that he's with so tell her what I said." She hung up before I could even protest. I shook my head and laughed.

"Moms is crazy," I told her

"What did she say?"

I replayed the phone call and Mercedes busted out laughing. She knew my mom was just as blunt as she wanted to be. She didn't bite her tongue for anybody. She never did and I knew she wasn't going to start now.

"Do you plan on telling her before Thanksgiving?" she asked me.

"Nah, she can find out right along with everyone else. She'll be alright," I assured her. My mother could have all the dreams she wanted but nobody outside of Sha, Cedes and I would be finding out before we received the ultrasound showing our little one was straight.

Cedes and I finished cooking together, ate and prepared

for our workweek. My crew was getting one of the biggest shipments we had ever received coming through. It was right before the holidays and I knew my boys would be down for making more money for their families. I kept my hands as clean as I could. I simply overlooked a few workers to count the work as it came in and how they bagged it up for trap distributions. Each trap had its own head honcho who was responsible for the oversight of work being broken down and bagged up properly. Junior picked up the money from each trap and Jay and I counted it to ensure it was right. I had no problems having a nigga laid out for my money being short. I didn't play about two things, my family and my dough. I busted my ass too hard to be shorted or tried by a greedy ass nigga.

By ten that night, Cedes was passed out and I was up watching the Giants play the Panthers. For some reason, I could not sleep. I knew it would be a long day if I wasn't able to get at least an hour of sleep. I did something I hadn't done in a long time. I prayed for the health of Cedes as well as the health of our unborn.

It was as if that prayer was enough to make me tired. Shortly after, I drifted off into dreamland.

*****

The next morning, the sound of running water woke me

up. I shifted my slight hard-on, stretched and climbed out of bed. As I walked closer to the bathroom door, I could hear Cedes throwing up. This was the part of pregnancy that I wasn't looking forward to for her sake.

"Are you okay, baby girl?" I asked as I walked over and rubbed her back.

"I don't know. I feel like shit."

She stood up, grabbed her rag and wiped her mouth. She grabbed the mouthwash and rinsed her mouth out.

I kissed the side of her face.

"It's worth it though," she sighed. "Good morning to you though."

"Good morning."

I walked around her and relieved myself before washing my hands and brushing my teeth. Cedes walked back into the bedroom and started getting ready for work.

"Do you want breakfast?" I questioned as I made my way back into the bedroom.

"I don't know if I'll be able to hold it down. I'll take something light like toast or a bagel."

I headed down to the kitchen and popped a few pieces of bread in the toaster. I preferred for her to eat a fuller breakfast, but I knew we would have to adjust to this new lifestyle depending on what the baby liked. Twenty minutes later, Cedes made her way downstairs with her oversized Michael Kors purse.

I buttered her toast, grabbed a can of ginger ale out of the fridge, and slid it across the island.

"Thanks, babe," she said as she dropped the soda in her purse. "Maybe if you're free, we can do lunch."

"Of course. Let me know when your free hour is and what you want, and I'll bring it up."

"Sounds good." She walked around and gave me a sensual kiss.

"Don't start or you'll be late to work," I teased her.

"Maybe instead of food for lunch, I'll take a quickie."

She winked and blew me a kiss before she turned and walked away. I chuckled and watched her strut out of the house. I walked to the door and watched as she pulled out. Once she was out of my sight, I ran upstairs to get myself dressed. Before I headed to the offices, I needed to stop by a few traps.

I loved making pop up visits. I loved catching niggas off guard. They never expected it and it also let me see who slacked and who actually worked.

I stopped over on Potters and saw a few little niggas standing outside. Once the young buck Julian spotted my whip, he jogged over. I rolled my window down and dapped him up.

"What's good around here, youngin'?" I questioned.

"Nothing. It's still early so shits a little slow, but you know it'll pick up. Plus, it's early in the month, so them fiends still have their checks and shit. You know how that goes."

I nodded.

"A'ight. Junior should be dropping some shit off to you later on this week. Stay up."

I dapped him up again, rolled up my window and pulled off. I stopped off at a few more traps before heading to the gas station I owned in the hood. My main reason for having so many legit businesses is because I wanted to offer as many legit jobs to young black males and females as I could.

I walked inside, grabbed a drink out of the freezer and went behind the counter.

"Hi, Mr. Washington," the cashier greeted. I truthfully had no idea who this young girl was.

"What's up? What's your name?"

"Tonya."

"When did you start?"

"Last week. Your brother hired me."

I nodded.

"How you like it so far?"

"It's not bad. It gets busy with the morning rush hour with people coming in and out for snacks, drinks and some for gas. Then in the afternoon with the kids getting out of school and thinking this is a hangout spot," she chuckled. I knew what she meant. We were located smack dead in the hood.

"Cool. Seems like you have everything handled. Did Sha leave the emergency contacts?"

She pointed to a little index card she had hanging on her side of the lottery ticket display.

"A'ight, if you need anything or have any issues, don't hesitate to call."

She smiled and nodded. I slapped two dollars on the counter and headed out. I knew I didn't have to pay for anything, but I always did.

I ran by the leasing office at the apartment complex we ran. I checked to see if any maintenance needed to be done. Michelle, the girl who I hired as the leasing agent, ran down how the tenants had been and if anybody needed notices for late payments or evictions. I hated having to evict people but some folks legit thought they were gonna get by without paying anything. It wasn't about the money; it was the principle. Until you own your own house with no bank loan, you gotta pay where you lay. Before I knew it, it was eleven-thirty and Cedes was about to go on her lunch hour. I quickly ran over to Subway to grab us some sandwiches and headed to her job.

Chapter Seven

Mercedes

I had just dropped my class off to the gym when I felt my phone vibrate in my purse. I knew it was nobody but Kas. It wasn't very often that we had lunch together but sometimes if he could get away, he would come up to the school and have lunch with me. I grabbed my phone and saw that he said he was outside. I walked out of the front of the building and hopped into the car with him. I leaned over and planted a kiss smack dead on his lips.

"How's your day going?" he asked as he parked.

"I can't complain. The nausea went away thankfully. You know we don't have to eat in the car, right? We can go to the classroom," I told him.

"A'ight." He killed the engine and we walked back towards the school. We stopped by the main office so that he could sign in and grab a visitor's pass before we headed to my classroom. "I love the way you have your class set up, ma. It's dope."

I smiled.

"Thanks. I take pride in keeping it nice. If we finish our activities early today, I'm going to do something for Thanksgiving. I printed out a couple of cornucopias with fruits for them to color and glue so that I can change the Halloween decorations on the wall."

We sat at the table that I used to correct papers as we ate and talked about random things.

"Aye, did you try and make an appointment with the doctor?" he asked.

"No, but I can try now," I told him as I pulled out my phone. I dialed the number to the clinic and hoped that they answered. Luckily, they did have an open spot and within ten minutes, I had my first appointment scheduled for the following week. Kas and I enjoyed the remainder of my lunch hour and before I knew it, it was time for me to go and get my class back from the gym. I planted a kiss on his lips and walked him to the front of the school. I headed down the hall to the gym to get my class.

The rest of the day flew by. As I climbed into my car, my phone rang. I twisted my face as I realized it was Shanie. *What the hell does she want?* I thought to myself.

"Hello," I answered.

"Hey, Cedes."

"What's up?"

"What are you up to?"

"Um, I'm leaving work." I was now genuinely confused by the point of this conversation. "What's up?" I repeated.

"Nothing, I was just calling to see what you were up to."

"Shanie, we aren't that cool," I said as I climbed into the car. "Especially for you to call me up randomly. You've never even called me when you were fuckin' with Sha, so why the hell are you calling me now?"

"I see you still think your shit doesn't stink. We'll see how you feel about that." She hung up before I could even say anything else. I shrugged her call off and headed home. I wasn't about to deal with her shit. She wasn't about to stress me out.

*****

Two Weeks Later...

Thanksgiving morning was here and Lex, my mother, Kayla, Kas' mother, Justine and myself were busy in the kitchen. I sent Kas to hang with Sha and stay out of our way. Justine was basting the turkey as Lex peeled potatoes and sweet potatoes and I cleaned greens with my mother. We were all making small talk with each other, as I was growing anxious and excited to share our news. I hoped that Rari could get his son and join us, but we knew how Janayah could be.

I was happy with the relationship that my mother and Kas' mother created. They seemed to be the best of friends, which was amazing because it made holidays easier to join together. I hoped they would both be equally excited when we shared that we're expanding our family by three.

Yep, that's right; Kas and I found out that we were having triplets. It came as a complete surprise. I was praying for one healthy baby and so far, I had three. I was further along than I anticipated, being twelve weeks. I never worried when my period skipped because it was irregular anyway.

Two of the babies were identical and one had its own sac. I prayed for Kas' sake that at least one was a boy, but whatever God blessed us with, I was fine to take. I made sure to take everything easy. Kas wanted me to stop working but unless the doctor placed me on high risk, that wasn't happening. I enjoyed my job and my class too much and I couldn't imagine being home all day, every day. I got bored way too easily.

Several hours later, dinner was done, and I watched as my house filled with so much love. I glanced around at the table as everyone grabbed a seat. I loved seeing our family come together as well as it did. I couldn't help but smile as I watched Rari help his son eat. My brother had become so mature since his son was born. Most people, when they entered relationships, worried about whether or not their families would get along but that was never an issue of mine. Off the back, my parents and Kas' parents clicked. Rari looked up to Kas and Sha.

Before I knew it, Kas squeezed my hand, signaling that it was time for us to share our news. I took a deep breath before speaking.

"Can I have everyone's attention?"

Everyone stopped talking and I didn't miss the side-eye that Mama Justine gave me. I tried to suppress my smile, but it was becoming harder.

"Kaseem and I are proud to announce that in May, we will be welcoming three bundles of joys."

"Three?" Justine stated as she jumped out of her seat. My mother's hands flew over her mouth and my father started coughing. "Oh my God!" Justine had tears in her eyes. My mother walked around to my side of the table and placed her hands on my stomach.

"I knew I was having those fish dreams for a reason," Justine shouted. "It's about damn time! I was getting jealous of Kayla's ass having a grandchild and here I was dreaming about fish and your asses couldn't tell me she was pregnant!"

"We wanted it to be a surprise, ma," Kas chuckled.

"Truthfully, I was starting to think y'all asses wasn't even fuckin' anymore," Justine blurted out. Kas and I couldn't help but laugh because Justine was something else. As everyone basked in the news and congratulated us, the doorbell rang, breaking us from our celebration. I excused myself and headed to answer. I got the surprise of my life when I opened the door and found three officers standing there.

"Can I help you?" It was as if I were riding a roller coaster the way my stomach dropped.

"We are looking for Kaseem Washington. Is he here?"

"Can I ask the reason you're looking for him?" I questioned.

"We have a warrant for his arrest," the first officer stated. I read the name on his tag and saw his last name was Croy.

"For what?" I snapped. I was sure Kas and them had

heard me, but this shit really couldn't be happening right now.

"Cedes, what's going on?" Kas asked coming up behind me.

"Kaseem Washington?" the officer spoke.

"That's me."

"You're under arrest for the illegal trafficking of firearms and possession and delivery of narcotics."

"WHAT?" I shouted. This had to be a mistake. Trafficking of firearms and selling drugs? What the fuck was really going on?

Chapter Eight

Kaseem

This shit couldn't be fuckin' happening right now! I was clean as fuck with everything I did and didn't touch shit. This could only mean that somebody's mouth was fuckin' running and I was gonna find out who it was.

I shook my head, kissed Cedes cheek and turned around for the officers to cuff me. I knew Cedes had a million and one questions and although I didn't want to at the moment, I guess it was time to answer her questions the next time we talked.

"Sha," I called out as I started walking backwards. "Call Jay and tell him what's up. He'll know what to do."

I looked at Cedes again who was crying and confused, blew her a kiss and walked out. I hoped Sha didn't open his mouth to explain shit because this was something that Cedes had to hear from me. I didn't utter a word as they placed me in the car, and we headed downtown. They weren't getting a word out of me without my lawyer, Tanika, who was Jay's sister.

Four hours later, they had me sitting in the interrogation room trying to instill fear in me. It wasn't working. All of the numbers they were throwing at me, trying to say I was looking at so many years was going in one ear and out the other. The fact that they were stalling on giving me my phone call let me know they really didn't have shit. I did want to know who was talking though. They wouldn't tell me, but I knew if I didn't find out, Tanika would when she got the papers.

An hour later, I was able to make my call. I took a deep breath as I dialed Cedes' phone number. I knew she was about to run off a mile a minute at the mouth. Once the operator was done with talking, I heard Cedes' voice come through the phone and it was like music to my ears.

"Are you okay?" she asked. I could tell she had been crying.

"I'm good, ma. Are you okay? I don't need you

stressing."

"It's so hard Kas. Today turned out to be shitty as hell. Here it is damn near ten at night and you're locked up like some animal. What the hell were they talking about anyway?"

"I have no idea but Jay's sister Tanika will find out. I shouldn't be here long at all."

"I hope not," she sighed. "I miss you already."

"I'll be home before you know it."

Before we even realized it, the twenty-minute call was ending.

"I love you, mama," I told her. "I promise I'm gonna figure everything out and get out of here." There was more meaning to what I was saying than what she knew.

"I love you more, Kas. I'll be waiting."

She blew me a kiss and the call disconnected. I hung it up and headed back to the holding cell. Normally, people would make that one phone call to their lawyer, but I knew Sha had that shit covered so I wasn't worried about it. I felt bad for pulling Tanika away from her family on Thanksgiving, but I paid her for situations like this. Therefore, it was time for her to earn her pay.

As I laid back in the holding cell, my mind began wandering. Where the fuck was my cousin, Andre and why the fuck didn't he put a bug in my ear that this shit was even happening? Something wasn't right and someone was playing dirty. I knew I wouldn't get another call, so I just decided to wait until tomorrow. I knew by then I would get some answers.

*****

The Next Day...

"Washington," an officer called. "Court, let's go." I stood up and stretched as I walked out of the holding cell. I felt dirty as fuck and wanted nothing more than to take an hour shower to wash this dusty ass holding cell smell off of me. The officer cuffed me and guided me outside to the bus that was taking me over to the courthouse. I was sure Tanika would be there and Cedes too. I didn't want her too because I didn't know what was going to happen. I didn't want any added stress on her that didn't need to be on her.

An hour later, it was my turn to face the judge. Scanning over the crowd, there she sat in the front row. Mercedes had a pair of Gucci shades covering her eyes and her hair thrown up in a loose ponytail but to me, she looked sexy as fuck. I gave her a small smirk before taking my seat behind the table waiting for the judge to begin. I took a deep breath.

"All rise," the bailiff spoke. He introduced the judge and

we all sat down. The judge ran down the charges and I cringed at each and every single one. Everything he said was true, but I was sure these fuckas had no proof.

"Your honor, I'm requesting for all of these charges to be thrown out as my client has nothing to do with this. None of the papers I've received from the officers have any solid proof my client has anything to do with it. My client is a legitimate tax-paying business owner. He is not the man that these gentlemen are trying to make out. If you aren't willing to throw the case out, then I'm asking that my client be released on bail."

The judge cut his eyes over at the cops. I'm sure he was pissed that these idiots wasted their time with their bullshit ass charges. The judge had asked them to approach the bench. I looked back at Cedes and gave her a small smirk. I knew I was about to walk out of here. After a few minutes, Tanika walked back over to me and whispered in my ear that everything was good.

"Due to lack of *evidence*," the judge emphasized evidence, "I'm throwing this case out. Mr. Washington continue to keep your nose clean. We need more men like you."

I had to hold my scoff. *If only you really knew,* I thought to myself. He banged his gavel and I was led to the back to wait for bail to be posted. Cedes had access to all of my accounts so the amount of bail wouldn't even matter. Thirty minutes later, I was released. I found Cedes down in the lobby waiting for me.

"Hey, beautiful." I scooped her up into my arms and spun her around. "How much did bail end up being?"

"Nothing. They released you on your own personal recognizance," she stated as we walked hand in hand out of the courthouse. "I have a question."

"What's up?"

"Are you into anything illegal?"

"Where did that come from?"

"I'm not dumb, Kaseem. They aren't going to come and arrest you with a warrant if they didn't have something."

"You just saw the case was dismissed, didn't you? That means they have nothing."

I made a mental note to ask Tanika who was on the paperwork.

"That doesn't mean shit. I may not have been raised in the streets, but I'm not completely green to the bullshit either. When they cuffed you, your face remained calm, but fire danced in your eyes. If you're hiding anything, it's best you tell me yourself rather than me find out through someone else."

She climbed into the car and didn't speak another word the entire ride home. *You gotta tell her man. Tell her before someone else does,* I thought to myself. I pulled out my phone and shot Jay a text.

Me: *Yo, hit Nika and ask her who was on those papers.*

I dropped my phone in my lap and closed my eyes. I played different ways to spill the shit to Cedes without it seeming as bad as it truly was, and I was drawing a damn blank.

Jay: *She said Shandra Calhoun.*

I know it ain't who the fuck I think it is. I ran my tongue across my teeth and counted to ten.

Me: *Yo Sha, what's Shanie's last name?*

If it was Shanie, the bitch was as good as fuckin' dead and I was pulling Sha away from the street shit. That pillow talking shit will have a nigga doing football numbers or staring at the roof of a church. I didn't know about anybody else, but I didn't want that shit.

Sha: *Calhoun, what's up?*

I had to count to ten again. I wanted Cedes to speed the fuck up and get home. I had to give Sha a mothafuckin' earful. That bitch had to fuckin' GO!

Ten minutes later, Cedes pulled into the driveway.

"I'm going to meet Lex and do a little Black Friday

shopping to ease my mind," she said.

"A'ight ma, take it easy and call me if you need anything," I told her. She nodded and I planted a kiss right on her lips. I watched as she pulled out and headed inside. I dialed Sha's number and he answered on the second ring.

"What's good, bruh?"

"Yo! Why is Shanie running her fuckin' mouth? What the fuck did you tell her, Shaheem?"

"W-what?" he stuttered.

"Don't fuckin' play dumb. What the fuck did you tell her?"

"Not much, but she did ride with me a few times."

I washed my hands across my face.

"Fuck man. She needs to go the fuck on vacation or some shit," I started speaking in code. Sha knew what I meant. Shanie needed to be pushing flowers out of the dirt. And that shit needed to happen sooner rather than later.

Chapter Nine

Mercedes

Kas was hiding something and I knew it. I had a feeling it had something to do with those damn charges they hit him with. Things were starting to make sense in my mind. Was Kas using these legit businesses to clean money from his illegal dealings?

Nah, he couldn't be.

My mind was racing, and I needed somebody to talk too. While waiting for Kas to be released, I had let his mother and my mother know that he was straight, but I let Justine know that I was coming to see her. If anybody knew Kas, it was his mother. I did plan to go shopping with Lex, but that wasn't until later. I pulled up to Justine's house fifteen minutes later and she was sitting on her porch reading a book.

"Hey baby girl," she greeted when I got out of the car. I walked up, hugged her and sat next to her on the swing.

"Would you ever lie to me?" I asked her cutting straight to the chase.

"Huh?"

"Come on, Mama. You know you heard me," I said giving her a knowing look.

She sighed. "What do you wanna know?"

"Is Kas into anything illegal?"

Her face said everything. No words needed to be said. My man was a gun trafficking fucking drug dealer. I put my head in my hands and started crying.

"Why are you crying?" she asked me.

"I thought that I knew Kaseem, but the truth is I have no idea who that man is."

"Mercedes don't do that. Don't make Kas out to be a bad person because he's not."

"He's a liar! For three years he put on a façade of being somebody he's not."

"Kas is exactly who he has been to you. The loving, caring, respectful young man that I raised him to be," she explained.

"There's a whole other side of him that you're forgetting."

"Listen," she said placing her hand on my knee. "Go talk to him and tell him to explain everything. I can't tell you certain things because only Kaseem has the answers that you're looking for."

I sniffled, wiped my face and took a couple of deep breaths.

"Okay. Thanks, Mama."

I hugged her again before I hopped back in my car. I was no longer in the mood to shop. Kaseem was giving me the answers I wanted, and I was getting those answers today.

Twenty minutes later, I walked into the house and found Kas flipping through channels in the living room. I walked over to the TV and pressed the power button then crossed my arms across my chest and glared at him.

"Okay, what did I do?" he asked looking confused.

"Kaseem Montrel Washington, I'm not going to ask you again, so I suggest you keep it a buck with me right now. Are you a gun trafficking drug dealer?"

He washed his hands over his face while taking a deep breath.

"Can you sit down?"

"Can you answer my question?" I countered.

"Yes and no."

"What the fuck does that mean?"

"Yes, I'm a gun trafficker, but no I'm not a drug dealer. I'm a kingpin."

My heart rate sped up. I couldn't believe he was admitting this shit to me. I sat down on the couch and shook my head. I got the answer I needed from Justine, but to hear him admit it was something completely different. I truly had no idea who I fell in love with.

"Why? I just don't get it. You risk your freedom when you own several legit fuckin' businesses. We're startin' a fuckin' family and if you for one-minute think that I would allow guns and drugs around my children, you've lost your mind!"

"Mercedes stop! When have you ever had me gone for more than eight to ten hours a day? I come the fuck home every night at a decent hour. We eat dinner together every night and breakfast together damn near every morning. I don't touch anything, and I haven't since well before I met you. I have workers for everything. Truthfully, all I do is count money with Jay," he explained.

"Jay? Jay's in on this too? That mothafucka smiled in

my face and knew what you were doing? Who else knew?"

He sighed again.

"Sha, Jay, and Junior are down with me. Tanika is Jay's sister; she knows. That's why she was right there when Sha called. My moms know. She doesn't approve and never did, but she understood why Sha and I did what we did."

"So, tell me why," I said sitting back on the couch.

He looked at me then down at the floor before he began speaking again.

"When I was twelve and Sha was ten, my moms got knocked. She was bringing a package out of state to one of my pops' workers while pops handled business back home and she got busted. When she spoke to my pops, he told her to give his name and he would take the rap because he needed her to be home raising his sons. He didn't need nor want her locked up. She did what he said, pops went down for eight years for the two packs moms had gotten knocked with. Pops left moms money, but with the back and forth to the prison out in Mass, keeping money on the books and raising two kids, moms began to struggle once the money was drying up. I never saw my parents struggle and I wasn't about to start. Pops was gone for about two years when I realized how moms would sit at the kitchen table in damn near tears each month tryna pay bills. I knew she probably wanted back into the drug life, but she promised my pops she would stay away.

"One day, I went and visited my pops, told him what was going down and I wanted in on what he was doing on the streets. He was hesitant, but he told me he would do it under one condition; I had to move smart and find ways to clean my money the legit way. He told me to come up with a business plan that would work. I planned and plotted for about three weeks before an idea came to me. Moms had great credit, so I had her apply for a business loan. She was approved and opened up one of the laundry mats. Once pops got wind, he put me in contact with one of his people and from there it was history. I tried to keep Sha away, but it was hard. Moms wasn't happy, but she knew there was no stopping us. When my pops got out, he and my mom sat me down and told me I was to keep my hands as clean as possible in order to be successful and remain on top. My pops never wanted back in, but I did put a couple businesses in him and moms name to keep their money flow right.

"Now, by no means am I saying that I'm right, and yes, I should have told you a long time ago, but I wanted to keep you as green to the streets as long as possible. I'm sorry, ma for not telling you. I truly am. I promise I haven't touched any type of drug or gun in years and I don't plan on it. My hands are clean, but I do oversee the illegal operations though," he explained.

I couldn't believe everything he had just said. It was a lot to swallow and I now had to consider if I wanted to be with this type of person. I loved Kas, and that was without saying. I just didn't know if this lifestyle was one, I wanted to continue to be a part of anymore.

Chapter Ten

Kaseem

Cedes sat there saying absolutely nothing. My heart was breaking as I stared into her eyes. The pain was evident in her eyes and it was killing me.

"Say something, Ma."

"Like what? I'm still trying to take all of this shit in. I feel like I'm a part of a lifestyle I never even knew existed. I'm out here spending drug money and shit. I didn't sign up to be a fuckin' hustla's wife," she snapped.

"You're not a hustla's wife, Mercedes. You're the wife of a businessman. None of the money you ever came across, was dirty. That shit is cleaned through my businesses before they even hit the accounts."

She shook her head.

"First of all," I began speaking again. "I need for you to calm down. Here we have the blessing we've finally been waiting for and I don't want you to do anything to risk or lose our blessing."

"You didn't care about these blessings when you were doing what you were doing," she scoffed. I let out a deep breath and began rubbing my temples.

"Mercedes, listen to me." I'm sure she knew I was getting frustrated by my tone. "I didn't get into this shit because I fuckin' wanted too. I did what the fuck I had to do for my family. My mother went from seeing thousands a week to living off of small savings that she put aside for rainy days. Did you think a nine to five was going to be able to keep up with that lifestyle? Pay for that mortgage she had for the house she lives in? Keep pops books stacked *and* raise two growing boys? No! So, as her oldest son, and the man of the house, I did what the fuck I had to do. My main focus was making sure my family was good, which is what I've been doing for the past fifteen years. I already told you the why. I can't change what I've done but it's who I am."

"What are you saying I have to just accept it?"

"Mama, I can't make decisions for you, but I respect any decision you make."

"If I asked you to walk away, would you?"

I sat silently for a minute. Truthfully, her question threw me for a loop. I had to think about an answer.

I sighed. "Yes."

She nodded her head.

"Cedes, I'm still the same man you fell in love with. Don't look at me any differently. Businessman Kas and Kingpin Kas both love you all the same."

"Tuh," she scoffed again. "You're a liar is what the fuck you are." I couldn't be mad at her for being mad at me. "If you think for one second that I'll raise my kids around drugs and guns, you're crazy."

I sighed deeply and thought of the words to say. I thought about what to say to her but truthfully, nothing I could say would change this image of a monster she had created.

"I gotta get away from you," she said as she stood up. My mind was yelling for me to stop her, but my feet wouldn't move. My heart wanted her to stay but I knew there wasn't anything I could say at this moment that would make her stay. "You're not even gonna say anything?"

"There's a lot I wanna say but no matter what I say, you

don't wanna hear it. Your mind is made up. Do I want you to leave? Absolutely not but I'll never hold you where you don't wanna be. If you need some time to decide what you wanna do, I'll give you that. Whatever you decide, I'll respect and if your decision is to leave, then just know I'll always take care of you and my kids."

I watched a lone tear slide down her cheek. She shook her head and walked off. I sat back and thought about what the fuck was happening. Twenty minutes later, Cedes came downstairs with her Louie duffle bag slung over her shoulders. We locked eyes briefly before she walked out. I sighed. Times like this I wished I had an older sister because, in this moment, I needed some female advice.

I picked up my phone and dialed my mother. She answered on the second ring.

"How'd it go?" she answered.

"Huh?"

"I was expecting your call," she said.

"How and why?"

She sighed, "Mercedes came by earlier asking about what you do. I told her that was a conversation she needed to have with you. It's not my place to have that conversation with her."

"You could've given me a heads up," I told her.

"Anyway, she left."

"She what?"

"She left," I repeated. "I don't know for how long or anything. I just know she packed a bag and left. I don't even know what to do," I admitted.

"Give her time. You just dropped a major bombshell on her and plus, she's pregnant so her hormones are raging."

I sighed. "I guess you're right."

"Let me ask you something, son. Why did you never tell her?"

"Honestly, I didn't know how. I love Mercedes with all of my heart. I guess the thought of losing her always made me feel like it was never the right time. I mean it's never easy admitting shit like that. Cedes makes a nigga want better but the amount of money I make from my business isn't something you just walk away from," I explained.

Just then, my front door opened, and the call disconnected. Looking over my shoulder, I spotted my mother closing the door behind her.

"Hey ma," I greeted as I slid my phone on the coffee table.

"Hey. Now, what were you saying?"

I sighed and repeated myself.

"If she loves you, she'll stay."

"I can't say that ma."

"Why?" she asked.

"Because not everyone is cut out to deal with this lifestyle. We," I said, pointing to her and myself. "We're used to this shit. Cedes wasn't raised in this environment. I tried to keep her away from this shit."

"How did she find out?"

"Your son can't keep his mouth shut. Pillow talkin' to Shanie and the moment they split, she started singing like a fuckin' canary. I told your son about his pillow talkin'. That shit could get a nigga football numbers."

"You got him into this shit," my mother snapped.

I cut my eyes at her.

"The same way you got me into this shit," I responded.

"Excuse me?"

"Cut it out, Ma. You're quick to try and blame me for the shit with Sha but you won't take some responsibility for me even gettin' into this shit!"

"Now hold the hell up Kaseem. I always have been against you going into this shit."

"But you never tried to stop me. You were used to the bread pops brought in. When the money started dwindling, what the fuck did you do? What steps did you take to keep shit going? You didn't try and find a job. You didn't pick up a hustle. You sat back and cried about shit that tears weren't gonna fix. As a mom to two boys, any woman would have shed some tears, put her family on her back and carried that shit until she made some shit happen. You knew with pops being a hustler, one of us was bound to follow in those steps if worse comes to worst."

I never imagined going off on my moms the way I was, but I was sick and tired of her blaming me for Shaheem's doings.

"The difference between me and you, I never wanted this shit for myself or Shaheem! I did this shit because I had to, and I saw that you weren't doing anything. I did everything I had to, to carry my family on my back. I had dreams, mama! You knew that. When you saw what I was getting into, you claimed you didn't like it, but that didn't stop you from spending and reaping the benefits. Not once did you try and take that load off of me. Not once did you try and divert Sha into a different lifestyle. All you did was bitch at me for so-called getting him into this lifestyle. If you're gonna blame me for Shaheem, then you gotta accept responsibility for me."

Mama was shedding tears and part of me felt bad, but I didn't regret it. I owned up to my shit, but mama had to own her shit too.

I sat back on the couch and took a few deep breaths before speaking again.

"Whether I put him on or not, Shaheem was gonna get into this shit. I never wanted him involved but if he was gonna be in this shit, I would rather him under me than with a random that could set him up at any given time. That's one thing he won't have to worry about with me," I explained. "But none of that gives him the right to start pillow talkin'. You're married to pops and he kept you out of the shit for a long time. I've been with Mercedes for years and she knew nothing. That's for a reason. The last thing I want is my lady lying to the law for me. The less she knew, the better."

"I understand all of that son, trust me, I do. I'll talk to Shaheem and let him know the shit he could possibly have caused with this," my mom said.

"Ain't no possibly caused. My pregnant girlfriend just left me."

"You're gonna have to accept some responsibility for that too. You're the one who lived the double life. Handle that shit with your lady and decide what it is you're gonna do." I cut my eyes at her, but she was right. It was my fault for keeping it from Cedes for so long. I just blamed Shaheem because had he not said anything, I wouldn't be dealing with this shit.

"Listen, son, I know how addicting this street shit is. Trust me, I do. But this shit is not worth your family. If you can't have both, let that street shit go." She stood up, walked over to me and kissed me on my forehead. She let herself out. I sat on the couch, lost in my thoughts.

Chapter Eleven

Mercedes

I drove around aimlessly for two hours. I was exhausted and hurt. I couldn't believe Kas had lied to me all these years. I truly felt like I had no idea who he was.

After driving for another thirty minutes, I went to Lex's house. I knew she would be wondering how everything was working out. I was ignoring everyone's calls and texts. Now that I knew, I truthfully didn't want to face anyone. I sighed and killed the engine outside of my sisters. I dialed her number as she answered on the third ring.

"I thought you were flakin' on our shopping trip," she

answered.

"I am," I said with a shaky voice. "Open the door."

She disconnected the call and opened the door seconds later. She came rushing down her front steps as I grabbed my duffle bag out of the backseat.

"Gimme that," she snapped. "Way too heavy for your ass to be carrying."

I chuckled and wiped my face.

"What's going on?" she asked the moment I crossed the threshold.

I sighed. There was so much to say but I had no idea where to start.

"It was all a lie, Lex! My entire relationship is based on a lie. Kas is everything they accused him of being. He's a fuckin gun traffickin' drug dealer," I cried. "How was I so blind to the bullshit?"

"Whoa! What?"

I ran down the conversation I had with both Kas and his mother.

"Wow. So, what are you gonna do?"

"That's the problem. I have no fuckin' clue! Lord knows I love Kaseem, but I love my babies more. It's my job as their mother to protect them. Even if that includes from their father. I'm a fuckin' teacher for crying out loud."

"Calm down, Cedes. Don't get yourself all worked up."

I put my head in my hands and cried.

"What am I supposed to do?"

Lex sighed. "Kas is the same man you fell in love with."

I rolled my eyes. "You sound just like him. The man I fell in love with was Kaseem the businessman."

"He still is! He just had more businesses then he shared."

"Whose side are you on here, Alexus?"

"The rational side. Think about it Cedes, you've never been placed in harm's way with what he does."

"That's not the point! He's out here risking his freedom for what? It's obvious they have a great income from the legit businesses so why continue the illegal shit?"

Lex sat quietly. It was a legit question that nobody could answer.

"I feel like I wanna give him an ultimatum but then I'll feel like an asshole."

"Cedes, for his family, I'm sure Kas would give the world. I can bet my last dollar he would do any and everything to continue to protect his family. Now I don't know much about Kas' businesses but I'm sure if he's lasted this long without getting caught, then he's doing something right," Lex said.

"So, I should let him keep hustling?"

"I say that you need to express your concerns and support what he chooses to do."

Part of me wanted to listen to Lex but the other part of me thought she sounded crazy as fuck.

"Just let me crash here for a few nights until I figure out what I'm gonna do."

"You can stay here as long as you need to sis. My house is your house."

Lex leaned in and gave me a hug. I needed it in that very moment. I knew Lex had a guest bedroom, so I made my way there while she went to her room. I just wanted to sleep off some of this stress. I would begin thinking about what I needed to do once I woke up.

*****

The Next Morning...

The vibration from my phone woke me up. Looking at the screen, I saw it was Kas calling. Rolling my eyes, I silenced the vibration before climbing out of bed. I was slightly confused, until I remembered the events of yesterday and how I ended up at Lex's house.

Going into the bathroom right outside of her spare bedroom, I handled my hygiene and relieved my bladder. I had to admit, these babies were doing a number on my bladder, but I refused to complain. I had never made it this far in pregnancy, so any ache, pain or discomfort moment, I would take with a grain of salt.

Leaving the bathroom, I ran into Lex coming out of her room.

"How are you feeling?" she asked.

I shrugged. "It's all a lot to process, ya know?"

"I get it. Just hurry up and call that man so he can stop calling me," she laughed.

I chuckled and shook my head as I headed back to the bedroom, I was staying in. Scooping up my phone, I saw the multiple missed calls and texts from Kas. Bypassing all of the texts, I tapped his name to dial his number.

"Hello," he answered sounding out of breath.

"Runnin' from the cops?" I asked.

"What?"

"Nothin'. What's up?"

"Nah, run that slick shit by me again," he said.

"Nothin' Kaseem. I'm just returning your millions of missed calls."

"See this is what I'm not tryna deal with Mercedes. I understand how you feel. I fuckin' get it. But you've known me for years and ain't never seen me have no run in with the law besides this last time. I was workin' out when you called, and I stopped to answer the phone."

"What did you want Kaseem?" I asked, skipping over everything he said.

"Nothin', it doesn't even matter. Whenever you're ready to talk, hit my line. You know the number."

Kaseem disconnected the call before I could even say anything. I was tempted to call him back, but my pride wouldn't let me. I was probably wrong for what I said but it slipped out faster than I could stop it. I couldn't help but question anything he said, and I knew if I couldn't trust him, then there was no more Mercedes and Kaseem.

Chapter Twelve

Kaseem
One Month Later...
Christmas Day

I was absolutely fuckin' miserable! The day I told Cedes everything, she told me she needed time, packed some shit and bounced. At first, I was calling and texting, but she was hardly answering. After she made the comment she made, I stopped reaching out and I couldn't. She only spoke through my mother and I hated every fuckin' second. From what she told my mother, she and the babies were doing good and she had found out the gender. Well, she had the scan, but she didn't know because she wanted everyone to find out together. To say that crushed me would be an understatement.

I mean I was glad that they were all healthy, but I wanted to be at every ultrasound appointment that she had and to learn that I missed one of the most vital ones, hurt me. We were set to have Christmas dinner along with gift exchanging at my mom's tonight. I was sure that Cedes would be there and I wasn't letting her leave until we at least talked. I couldn't go another fuckin' day without her being home. I missed my lady like hell.

I sighed as I climbed out of bed and dragged my ass to the shower. Without Cedes, I didn't do shit. I hardly left the house. I didn't even check in on the street shit like normal. I knew Jay and them would keep shit running. I took a twenty-minute shower, the majority of the time just allowing the water to run down my body. It was well after three in the afternoon and if my mother called me one more time, I was gonna lose my shit. She had expected me to be there for breakfast, but I skipped it.

I guess a nigga could admit that he was depressed as fuck. I had to shake this shit though because it wasn't me at all. I got dressed in some black Levi jeans, my Jordan Taxi 12's, a black and white checkered button-up and threw on some Louis shades. I may have looked like fly as hell, but inside I felt basic and damn near dead.

I needed my lady back.

*****

Later That Day…

By the time I made it to my mother's, it was well after six-thirty. I knew I was going to get an earful. I reached in the back and grabbed the gift bag I had of gifts. I smiled slightly when I noticed Cedes' Charger parked in the driveway. I could only imagine how big her belly had gotten and I couldn't wait to rub on it and talk to my babies. I put a little pep in my step as I headed inside.

I crept in slow and heard everyone in the living room. I peeked in and it was as if all eyes were on me. Everyone stopped talking but it wasn't long before my mother broke the silence.

"It's about fuckin' time! I thought I was going to have to send your father to your house and drag your ass out the fuckin' bed," she said as she stood up.

I smirked as I glanced around the room. My eyes landed on Cedes who had on a charcoal gray sweater dress with some Uggs. Her hair was bone straight but she had a small section pulled up into a ponytail on the top of her head. My eyes traveled down to her round belly. Any anger or hurt I felt, melted at the sight of my lady carrying my babies.

"Now we can do the gift exchange and then the gender

reveal for my grandbabies," she said as she walked over to the tree and sat on the floor. She started calling names and handing out gifts. I never expected anything but anybody but my parents always got me something.

I watched as everyone admired their gifts from my parents. I kept stealing glances at Cedes who was fighting to not make eye contact.

"Kas and Cedes, here, we got y'all something that's for the both of you," my mother spoke.

I didn't move as I watched her hand the gift to Cedes. She slowly opened it and out fell two tickets with a postcard clipped to the front. She picked them up off her lap and smiled as she flipped them around and a postcard with the word 'Bahamas' written across a clear ocean view was plastered. I smiled and shook my head.

"Ma, how are we traveling with three babies on the way?" I asked.

"Shit, I'll watch them while y'all go. Y'all stubborn mothafuckas need to go on a damn vacation. The shit's booked for like next July, but before you start questioning, how about a thank you?" she snapped.

I walked over to her.

"Thanks, mama." I kissed her on her cheek before handing out the couple gifts I picked up. This was where

Cedes came in because I was simple. Everyone got some sort of jewelry because it was the only thing I really knew how to shop for.

"Cedes," I called out. She looked at me for the first time. "Can I talk to you?" She didn't say anything as she got up and followed me. We headed out to my parents' back breezeway. "You look beautiful," I said starting up the conversation.

"Thank you. You don't look half bad yourself."

"Look, ma. I'm sorry. I miss you. I miss your cooking, I miss your conversation, I miss your laugh, I miss your smile; I just miss your all-around presence. The house and my life are so empty without you. Can you come home?" I know I probably sounded like I was begging but fuck it. I needed my lady back.

She sighed.

"I've done a lot of thinking and soul-searching. Would you be willing to give up that lifestyle if needed"?

"Mercedes, I would give up everything I had if it meant getting to have you and my babies. All I need is you. All I want is you." I meant every word I said.

"Keep your hands clean, Kaseem. I'm not playing. Any sign of you getting dirty, I'm taking my babies and I'm leaving."

I walked over and pulled her close to me. I rubbed her stomach as I planted kisses all over her face. Hand in hand, we walked back inside where my mother had everyone around a cake at the kitchen table.

"Alright y'all, I know Cedes brought the envelope with the gender to the bakery and had them do a three-layer cake. In between each layer is frosting and each color frosting represents the sex of the babies. Y'all ready to cut the cake?" my mom asked. Cedes and I walked over. Cedes grabbed the knife and wrapped my hand around hers as we sliced a piece.

"Oh my God!" Cedes shrieked. "We have…"

Chapter Thirteen

Mercedes

"Girls!" I screamed as I dropped the knife and instantly started crying. I couldn't believe this was happening. I just knew one of the babies was going to be a boy; at least for Kaseem's sake but nope, here we are having three girls. I wiped my face as my mother came and wrapped her arms around me. No matter how hard I tried, I couldn't stop the tears from flowing.

"You're having girls," my mother reiterated. I sniffled a few times and wiped my face. Looking up, I locked eyes with Kas who wore the biggest smile. I smirked as I walked into his awaiting arms.

"Three girls huh?" he questioned as he kissed my forehead. He hugged me tightly as I continued to cry. "No worries, we got this Ma. You still have plenty of time to give me my son." I snapped my head up and looked up at him.

"Son? Boy you crazy," I said wiping my face and pulling away from him.

"I'm fuckin' with you. I know this pregnancy alone is taking a lot out of you, so any future kids are on you," he said. Before I could even say anything else, Justine interrupted by squeezing in between us.

"Do you have names picked out?" she asked.

"Ma, she barely even has time to register that there are even three kids in her belly, never mind a name," Kas said.

"Listen, I'm not about to argue with y'all already," I chuckled. "I haven't even thought about it honestly, mama."

"Well we're about to get started on everything," Justine said pulling me away from Kas. With these three babies being the first granddaughters, I knew my daughters were about to be spoiled by everyone.

For the rest of the night, we enjoyed the company of the family. I couldn't lie, it felt good to be around love. I wasn't sure if I was 100% over the situation with Kas, but for the moment, I would forget about it.

*****

Four Weeks Later...

I waddled into my appointment ready for it to be over. Today wasn't a good day for me. I stayed a few nights with Kas but staying with him again, made me realize how much trust was gone. Every time we left the house, I questioned where he was really going. I drove myself crazier worried about his safety and I knew even though he said he would give up the streets, it wouldn't happen as fast as I wanted it too.

Between my hormones, my trust issues and this morning sickness that lasted all damn day, I was miserable. The only thing that brought me joy was feeling my girls move and knowing they were healthy. Riding the elevator, I thought about all I had to do to get ready for these girls. I hadn't had a baby shower yet, but I had already begun shopping for them and the room I was staying in at Lex's house was way too small. I refused to go back to the house with Kaseem. As much as I missed my house, too much was going on for me to go back. I made a mental note to look for an apartment for me and the girls.

After checking into my appointment, I sat in the waiting room and immediately wished they would call me back. I hated coming here because bitches acted like they never saw a woman pregnant before. I rolled my eyes at the chick sitting next to me. Before I could say anything to her, they called me to the back.

"How are you feeling today, Ms. Castro?" the nurse asked as she closed the door behind me.

"Large and irritable," I told her.

"Welcome to the joys of pregnancy," she joked. I smirked but didn't say anything else as she began taking my vitals. "Any swelling?"

"Sometimes my feet but when I elevate, it goes down."

She finished up my vitals before leaving, letting me know the doctor was going to be coming in. Within fifteen minutes, Dr. Hardaway walked in.

"Sorry it took me so long," she apologized. "How are you today?"

"I'm good; feeling large but good."

Dr. Hardaway chuckled before logging into her system.

"I see you told the nurse you're experiencing some swelling?" I nodded. "It's good that it's going away with elevation. Your next appointment we'll do your glucose test to check for gestational diabetes. One thing I can say, you probably will only last another ten or so weeks. It's normal to not go to forty weeks when pregnant with multiples," she explained. "If you don't go in by thirty-seven weeks, we'll look to induce you at thirty-eight weeks."

"What are the chances of them coming before thirty-seven weeks?"

"Very likely. In my experience, triplets tend to come by thirty-seven weeks. Based on your ultrasounds, they are all growing rather well and all within two to three ounces of each other. Go ahead and lay back so we can do measurements and heartbeats. Do we have to go get dad in the waiting room?"

A wave of sadness came over me.

"No, he's not here," I said swallowing the lump that formed in my throat. My stubbornness was stopping Kas from being as involved in this pregnancy, as he wanted to be but every time, I was around him, all I could think about was his lying.

"Oh... Okay."

I'm sure Dr. Hardaway knew something was up because Kas was just as excited as I was, if not more about this pregnancy yet he hadn't been to the last few appointments.

I couldn't stop the tears from falling as I listened to the strong heartbeats of my girls. Dr. Hardaway and I discussed what labor would be like and deliver. We were planning for a C-section although I wanted a vaginal delivery. One thing I did know was this was going to be my one and only pregnancy. All I had prayed for was one successful pregnancy and since I was getting that, I wasn't going to push my luck because I couldn't handle another loss.

Chapter Fourteen

Kaseem

Sitting in the driveway, I stared at the house I once shared with Mercedes. Nobody could tell me after Christmas that my girl wasn't bringing her ass home for good, but I was sadly mistaken. She spent a few nights, but she let it be known she wasn't coming back. I had done exactly what she asked; stayed out the streets, but it wasn't enough for her. To make matters worse, she notified me about appointments for the baby *after* the appointments were over. That shit hurt me to the core.

I sighed and climbed out of the car, heading into the house. Unlocking the door, I heard the TV on in the living room. Rounding the corner, I was surprised to see Mercedes sitting on the couch.

"Where's your car?" I asked her walking around the couch to sit in front of her.

"Garage," she answered flatly.

"What's wrong?"

She sighed heavily and began fiddling with her fingers, which was a clear sign something was bothering her.

"Cedes, talk to me, Ma."

She sniffled and wiped her face quickly. Sitting on the coffee table in front of her, I cupped her chin making her look at me.

"Don't shut me out. We've always been solid as one. Talk to me."

"I'm moving back in with my parents?"

"What?"

"I don't know if it's my hormones or if my trust is just really shot, but I can't shake the lie at all. Every time I try to move past it, I'm reminded of the embarrassment I faced having them cops come in and rip you from me. I don't want to have that stress while trying to maintain a healthy pregnancy. It's hard enough carrying three babies, I can't worry about you too. I'll always love you and that won't change, but I have to get over this on my own before trying to force myself to get over this for you."

I didn't have anything to say. Hell, I didn't know what to say.

"I respect it. I just ask that you stop shutting me out. These girls are just as much my kids as they are yours. Just because you're mad at me, don't shut me out of my kid's life. I don't deserve it and they don't either."

"So, you're just okay with ending us?" she asked ignoring what I said.

"No Mercedes, I'm not okay with it but what do you want me to do? I've been fighting to show you for the last two months. I've kept my hands clean like you've asked, but you've decided to ignore all of that. I don't know what the fuck else to do so I'm just gonna respect your wishes. I'm asking for you to respect mine."

"Do you not love me?"

"What kind of question is that? You got my heart and have had it for years. I love you enough to let you go because I know I fucked up. It was selfish of me to hide my dealings, but I did it to protect you. You're already stressed enough trying to bring three healthy babies into this world and I'm not about to add more stress. If we have to be apart for you to get through this pregnancy in one piece, then so be it."

Mercedes didn't say anything else. I honestly didn't know if I expected her to say anything else.

"One thing I want you to remember, if you need anything whether it be for yourself or the babies, don't hesitate to call. It's my job as a man to make sure you and my babies are good." She sniffled and nodded. "I also don't expect you to stay at your moms forever either. I know your parents' house is roomy but preparing for three babies isn't gonna be easy in one room so if you want your own place, let me know and I'll get right on it."

"Thank you, but I don't know if that would be smart. I'll be going in within the next ten weeks. I go for diabetes testing at my next appointment."

"You won't be forty weeks in ten weeks, why are you not going full term?" I asked

"Dr. Hardaway said it's normal to not go forty weeks with multiples, and they usually aim to deliver by thirty-eight weeks. She said if I don't go by thirty-seven weeks, she'll induce me at thirty-eight."

"Then we gotta get shit in place. Ten weeks will be here before either of us blink."

"I know. It kinda scared me when she said it, I'm not gonna lie. I just want healthy babies. I've been thinking about names," she said.

"Oh yeah? What you got?"

"Kashmere Mercedes, Kassidy Monroe and Kashlyn Marie."

"Not a fan of Kashlyn," I told her honestly.

"You have anything better?"

"Kaseema."

"Bye Kaseem," she laughed.

"Don't stop doing that," I told her as I stared at her.

"Doing what?"

"Laughing and smiling. You're glowing and when you laugh and smile, your glow stands out even more." I watched as she blushed and tried to look away from me. "Kassandra. Kassandra Marie."

"I like that," she smiled again.

Mercedes and I spent the rest of the night laughing and talking like old times. For once, it felt like old times, but it was short-lived when Cedes asked me to follow her to her parents' house at damn near one in the morning. Biting my tongue, I did as she asked. Once I made sure she got in safe, I headed down to 148 for a drink. I damn sure didn't want to be in the house, especially not alone.

After having four shots of Remy, I hopped and my car and headed to the crib. My mind instantly went to Mercedes and I wanted nothing more than to climb in the bed up under her. I tried to call her, but she kept sending my calls to voicemail. I sighed heavily before heading home. I didn't even make it in the house. Sitting outside in the car again, I dozed off.

*****

The Next Morning...

Knockin' on my window jolted me from my sleep. Pulling my gun from in between the seat and the center counsel and pointed it towards the window. Jay threw his hands in the air and took a step back. Lowering the gun, I opened the door to step out. I shook my head because I couldn't believe I had slept in my car.

"Damn nigga. Anybody could have blasted your ass out here sleeping in a car like you homeless and shit. You good?"

I stretched before hitting the alarm on my whip and heading inside with Jay in tow.

"Nigga I'm all fucked up. Cedes said she's not coming back," I admitted.

"So, what you gonna do?"

"I have no clue. I never expected her to dip."

"Then you wonder why I always told your ass to be real!"

"Don't start that shit, Jay. Had Shaheem's ass not been

pillow talkin', I would have been good. Keeping my business from my personal has always been easy, but Sha wanna start bringing untrustworthy bitches around."

"Nah don't do that Kas. Yeah, Sha was wrong for pillow talkin' with Shanie, but you gotta be man enough to accept where you fucked up. YOU kept that shit from Cedes knowing that when and if she found out, she would be gone. You chose to continue the façade. You gotta take that shit on the chin."

I couldn't even respond to Jay because he was right. I had to stop placing the blame in other places because ultimately, I didn't give Cedes the chance to decide if she wanted to be a part of this life but figured if she was with me, she would accept either life. Knowing the kind of girl Cedes was, she would have never given me the time of day. I was selfish and wanted her by any means necessary.

"I hear you. It is what it is though."

"So I'ma ask you again, what are you gonna do?"

"Get back to the money. I'ma go 100% legit but I gotta make a few more moves to secure more bread and then I'm stepping away. By the time my kids turn one, I gotta be done."

"Say less."

I dapped up Jay and he sat on the couch, turning on the

TV as I headed to hop in the shower. I couldn't mope around because Cedes left. I planned on hitting the streets, tying up these loose ends and getting the fuck up out the streets for good.

Chapter Fifteen

Mercedes
Five Weeks Later...

I tossed the pillow over my head trying to block out Ferrari's yelling on the phone. This was the downside with living with my parents; my brother was here too and had no regards for anyone trying to sleep. I couldn't lie, I was miserable as shit. The doctors pulled me off of work and put me on bed rest. I was cramped in this little ass room, and I could hardly sleep or make it to the bathroom. The majority of my days were spent moaning and groaning. Lex came by to visit daily after work to keep me company, but I was sure she was tired of hearing my complaining.

I slammed the pillow down and got out of bed.

Snatching the door open, Ferrari was pacing back and forth in front of my bedroom door on the phone.

"Are you fuckin' serious? You can't have this argument in your own room or somewhere else? People are trying to sleep," I snapped.

"It's one in the afternoon Mercedes. Get your ass up."

"I wouldn't give a shit if it was seven at night, keep your conversations to yourself!"

"Get your own fuckin' place and you can have all the peace and quiet you want," he said before walking down the stairs. I gritted my teeth and went to the bathroom. I had to get the fuck outta this house because Ferrari was gonna make me fuck him up with his mouth.

Once I finished in the bathroom, I grabbed my phone and shot Kas a text.

Me (1:13pm) – Can you link me with someone who has links to apartments? I gotta get outta here.

The moment I hit send, I regretted it. I knew Kas would do nothing but try and get me to come back home.

K's Daddy (1:15pm) – You have a whole house you could return too, but if you really want an apartment, give me a few hours to make some calls.

I didn't bother to respond. I rubbed my stomach as I felt the girls begin to move. I smiled as they did their gymnastics around each other. I grabbed a pair of leggings and a long sleeve oversized t-shirt from the duffle bag I had. While waiting for Kas to respond, I decided to go out and do some shopping since my baby shower was a week away. Everything was pretty much done; I just had to get some minor things and find a pair of comfortable shoes.

Once I got outside, I immediately realized my Charger would not comfortably fit three baby car seats. Hell, it barely fit me being pregnant. I shot Kas another text letting him know I would be swapping the Charger for the Lexus truck at his house. Kas had bought me the Lexus truck last year for Christmas but I always preferred the Charger unless it snowed.

Kas responded letting me know I could either take the Lexus truck or go to his dealership and upgrade the Charger to something else I wanted. I ignored that text because getting rid of my Charger wasn't going to happen. I loved this car. Eventually, there would be times that I wouldn't have the girls and when those times came, I would pull my baby back out. Before heading out to Wrentham to shop, I stopped by Kas' house to get the truck.

Pulling up to the house, I couldn't help but feel kind of sad. I missed my house. Everything in me was telling me to go back home, but with as bad as I was now with my emotions and hormones, I knew it wasn't a good idea. At least not right now. I opened the garage and was surprised to find an E Class Benz sitting there. I had never seen this car before. I twisted my face and killed the engine to the Charger and waddled up to the Lexus. I glanced at the car again. Starting up the Lexus, I dialed Kas' number on the Bluetooth.

"What's good, Ma?"

"Who's Benz?"

"Huh?"

"If you can huh you can hear me."

"I bought it for Sha for his birthday next week. Did you forget?"

Truthfully, I hardly looked at a calendar to see the date, so I didn't even realize Sha's birthday was coming up.

"Oh okay. Well when you get back, can you pull my Charger into the garage?"

"I'm out of town for another two days. Can you just pull it in before you leave?"

"Where are you?"

"Handling business," he responded. I didn't miss the female giggle in the background and my heart shattered. I immediately disconnected the call and couldn't help but cry. The thought of Kas being with another woman made me sick to my stomach.

I cried for what felt like forever until my eyes were dry and irritated. I backed out of the garage and put the Charger in the garage. Closing the garage, I pulled out my phone to text Kas.

Me (2:03pm) – the fact that you've already moved on and have a new female in your life lets me know either she's been there, or you never really loved me. I can't believe all it took was a little break for you to move on like I meant nothing. From now on, all communication will be done through Alexus. Have a nice life.

I blocked Kas' number and pulled away from the house we once shared. I felt like my heart was left on the ground of the garage and I honestly didn't know what to feel or think. I jumped on the highway and put on Keyshia Cole's *The Way It Is* album. I knew I didn't have hardly enough room for the shopping I was about to do but Kaseem's credit cards were about to feel my pain.

Within forty minutes, I was pulling into the outlets. Pulling up the credit card apps on my phone, I was glad to see he had paid them all and they all had a balance of zero.

"Thanks, baby daddy," I said out loud to myself. Just as I stepped out of the car, my phone rang. "Hey Lex," I answered.

"Bitch, don't *hey Lex* me. What the fuck is going on and why is Kas blowing up my phone like I'm his bitch?"

"I may have told him that all communication needs to go through you."

"Why? What is going on?" I sighed as I ran down the earlier conversation, I had with Kas. "Bitch you're acting petty, just like Janayah."

"Don't start the shit, Alexus. If he moved on, there is no need for us to talk."

"Yes, there is! You're having his kids Mercedes! One thing I can say is ever since you've been pregnant, your common sense is lacking. You immediately start pointing the finger and blaming rather than hearing him out. I'm not saying Kas is always right, but you aren't either Mercedes, and you need to realize that. You need to hurry up and give birth so you can get back to yourself."

I didn't respond to her right away. "I'll talk to you later," I told her before disconnecting the call. Just before I dropped my phone in my purse, a text came through.

Rari (2:53pm) – I'm sorry for snappin' out earlier. Janayah is on her bullshit so to have to deal with her and then to have you comin' out with an attitude, I just wasn't in the mood for it. I love you sis.

I told Rari he was fine and that I loved him too. I

dropped my phone in my purse and headed into the Adidas store first. I loved the fact that they were having a sale. By the time I was done, each of the girls had four matching Adidas tracksuit and one for me for when I dropped this load. I cashed out, grabbed the bag and headed to the Ugg store. Although I knew I didn't need anything else, retail therapy was definitely helping my mood and it made me even happier that it was on Kas' dime.

Chapter Sixteen

Kaseem

I dialed Cedes' number again just as I got another alert that the second credit card had been maxed out. Just based on the stores she was hitting, I could tell she was at Wrentham. I wasn't even mad at her maxing out the credit cards, I was mad that she was accusing me of some shit that wasn't true. I was out of town with Jay and Cedes happened to call while the waitress was taking Jay's order. I tried to explain that to her, but it was clear she added me to the blocked list.

Trying her phone again, I was met with the voicemail. I gave up and kicked back on the couch at the hotel we were staying in. Here we were on an important business trip, and I couldn't even focus. Jay let himself in my room and immediately started talkin' shit.

"Nah nigga. We not about to do this. We're here on business. Shake that shit off. Deal with that shit when you get home. Put your mind on what you came here for," he snapped. He was right. I was here to let my connect know everything was going through Jay moving forward. I thought long and hard about remaining in the game, but it wasn't worth it. A nigga wanted his family back more than ever. The thought of missing out on important shit in my kid's growing up had me ready to give it all up to be there.

"A'ight."

Jay sat down and rolled a blunt as we discussed how the meeting would go with Julio. Julio started off as my pops connect and was handed down to me. I knew he expected me to hand it over to Sha, but I couldn't do that. Sha wasn't fully built for this shit like I was and the situation with Shanie proved it. After that incident, I pushed Sha more into our legal businesses. I couldn't afford what I worked so hard to build and maintain, to go down due to carelessness. I knew Jay would run this shit with an iron fist, so I wasn't worried about shit happening with him taking over.

Three hours later, I was meeting Jay in the lobby of the hotel. I slid my black shades on as we made it outside and jumped into the Jaguar we rented. It didn't take long to pull up to the beach house that Julio owned. This was the first time I had been to his crib out here in Jersey. Usually, he came to Rhode Island to do business. I had to admit, I was in awe. Julio's crib was everything a hood nigga dreamed of. The house on the water was once my dream, but now I wanted nothing more than to be legit.

Before I could even activate the alarm, one of Julio's bodyguards was at the door waiting for us. He immediately patted us down as we reached the porch. Once we were clear, we followed him to Julio's basement. Julio was sitting at his cherry wood desk with an unlit cigar in his hand.

"Take a seat gentleman," he said as he stood to grab glasses and his bottle of whiskey. He poured us all a shot before taking a seat again. "How has Jersey been treating you?"

"Jersey's nice," I told him. "But I'm ready to get back to my city."

"I gotta admit, Providence is a beautiful city. I always enjoy coming to town – for several reasons."

"Speaking of those reasons, the reason I requested the

meeting is because…" I paused and took a deep breath. "I'm stepping down."

Julio placed his glass down and leaned back in his chair.

"What brought this about?"

"I have three kids on the way, Julio."

"Three? You've been a busy man, huh?" he chuckled.

"Nah, my wife is pregnant with triplets."

"Oh damn. You know you don't have to step down because you have kids? You won't be the first plug with kids and won't be the last."

"I had a close call already Julio and I was looking at football numbers. I can't run that risk. I've already put everything in place for a smooth transition."

"Are you keepin' it in the family with your brother?" Julio asked taking another shot.

"Yes and no. Yes, I'm keeping it in the family with my brother but not Shaheem."

"Then who?"

I nodded in Jay's direction.

"My brother Jay. He's been down with me since day one when I was hugging the block and every time I moved up in rank, he moved up. He will have the same team and operations will run the same, he will just be the head."

Julio nodded and puffed on the unlit cigar. The silence

in the room had me thinking Julio wasn't going to accept this.

"I'll tell you what. I have one of the biggest shipments coming in next month, over one hundred bricks. It'll be split between Providence and the new expansion to Boston. The traps in Boston are set up, you just have to go up there and make sure all of it gets there and have Jay meet the dudes out there. Jay, I hope you're ready because this Boston expansion is bigger than we ever could have thought.

"I'm ready," Jay assured.

I sat back and stared at Julio. I was expecting to just tell him I was done and walk away. The silence in the room was thick. I ran my tongue across my teeth and began nodding.

"A'ight. When is it coming in?"

"Both drops will be done by the second Wednesday of the month. My girl Nicki here will be up in Boston when y'all get there. It's her people who are going to be running shop up there. I basically just want them to know who Jay is, so they'll know who they'll have to go through when it comes time to re-up. They'll be doing the leg work; Jay will be their plug."

Jay and I nodded.

"Let's get this shit done," I said toasting with him and Jay. I was ready to get through this shit. It was time for me to get everything in order for my daughter's arrival.

Chapter Seventeen

Mercedes

The day of my baby shower was here, and I couldn't be happier. For the first time in weeks, I wasn't in pain. I woke up feeling refreshed and in a good mood. I waddled to the bathroom to handle my hygiene before going to grab food before heading to my hair and makeup appointments. Finishing up in the bathroom, the smell of frying bacon came through the house, causing my stomach to growl.

Entering the kitchen, I found my mother adding bacon to the plate she was making as well as pancakes.

"Good morning," she greeted.

"Hey, mama."

"How are you feelin'?"

"Good today. I'm ready to celebrate these babies and get ready for them."

"I'm nervous for all that you're gonna get on top of what you already have. How do you plan on housing gifts for three babies in your room?" she asked. I knew it was only a matter of time before the question came up. I couldn't help but feel that I was starting to take up space in my parents' house and although they love me, I know for a fact they did not want three babies under their roof.

"I'm going tomorrow to check out a place."

"I'm not kickin' you out, Mercedes."

"I know, but you're right and I've been thinkin' about it myself. My girls need their own and it's not ideal to share one room with three kids."

"Why not go back home with Kaseem? Are you all not together?"

"I don't know what we are honestly. I'm a mess, he's a mess and us being under the same roof will probably be horrible."

"Babies change everything, Cedes. Sometimes for the good and sometimes for the bad but it's up to the people in the relationship to determine if it's worth it," she said sliding my plate in front of me.

"I know and I know my hormones are out of whack. I gotta get back to me because, at this rate, shit will get bad."

"How does he feel about you getting your own apartment?" My mom sat at the opposite side of the table and began picking at her plate as I popped a piece of bacon in my mouth.

"He hates the idea of it. He says the same thing you said about going home. Believe me, I miss the hell out of my house, but one thing I know is I don't trust Kas and can't seem to let go of his lie."

"Mercedes, what exactly did he lie about?"

"Everything!" I snapped.

"Before this incident, did you ever ask him about what he did?"

"Yes, and he only told me about the legal businesses."

"But did you ask if he was into anything illegal? Has he ever put your life at risk? Was he not 100% honest when you did approach him about what he did?"

"No, I never asked before and yes when I asked him, he was honest. I expected that he would have been honest up front," I told my mother honestly.

She sighed. "I've sheltered you so much. Your uncle, my brother, was in the same business back in the day that Kas is in now. Now don't get me wrong, I hated it then as much as I hate it now, but I don't judge. Uncle Lamont told us as little as possible and he never told any of his women about what he did, unless he met them in that business. The less you know, the better. Now what I can say is the years I've known Kas, I can tell he moves smart. Had that incident never happened, I would have never guessed he was in that business. I hate that the incident was the way you had to find out, but I can almost guarantee you that he didn't tell you out of an attempt to protect you," she explained.

"I know, Ma but just imagine it would have come out different? I'm a schoolteacher and imagine seeing it blasted all over the TV for my coworkers to see that my man is a fuckin' kingpin. How could I explain to my boss that I knew nothing about it? How could I look my students' parents in the eyes and let them know I would protect their kids?"

"The same way you have done over the last few years, Mercedes! Again, I respect the fact that Kas has always kept that shit away from you. You were never at risk and your job was never at risk. You trusted him all these years. I can't see him changing any of that now; especially now with kids involved. If anything, the protection would be raised."

"So, you think what he was doing is okay?" I asked. It seemed as if nobody saw anything wrong with Kaseem being a kingpin.

"No, I don't think it was okay, but who am I to judge? Like I said, my brother was in the same game. Not on as large a scale as Kas, but he was into it. I'm sure after this, he'll get out, but I can't judge him for doing what he did. He also has legal businesses, so he can continue his legal hustle and care for his kids."

I nodded as I took in what my mother was saying. She was right. I think the major part of me that was upset that Kas hid it from me because it made me feel like Kas couldn't trust me. My biggest fear, especially since being pregnant, was losing Kas. Thanksgiving just proved that anything could happen.

"Mercedes, you are my child. I know you and you're miserable. Don't let your stubbornness cause you to lose your love," my mother said. "But enough of that. It's the big day. Go start getting ready because time is gonna fly before you even realize."

I finished off my food before heading to take a quick shower and head out. I turned Pandora on and stripped. Walking towards the bathroom, I caught a look at myself in the full body mirror on the closet door. I had to admit, I was huge, but looking at my stomach and knowing what my body was doing, made me smile.

Two hours later, I was pulling up to my hair appointment. Walking into the salon, it was packed and there wasn't a seat in sight. I immediately became annoyed but stood off to the side.

"Hey, Cedes," my girl Toya greeted. Toya had built a name for herself here in Providence with her magic hands. Between braiding and slaying blowouts and wigs, wasn't nobody touching her. She truly started from the bottom, braiding out of her kitchen to now, owning one of the biggest braiding and wig salons. My girl stayed booked and it was only a matter of time before she was doing shit for celebs.

"Hey boo," I waddled over to kiss her cheek.

"Girl, you look like you're about to pop at any moment."

"At this point, I'm over it. I'm tired and ready for them to be here," I told her honestly.

"Soon enough. Well first, you gotta get through today. I'm just about done with her and then I'm gonna get started on you."

"Alright cool."

"You getting your face beat too?"

"Yeah," I told her flipping through a magazine. "Lex told me about this dope makeup artist. I think her name is Margarita."

"She goes by @beatbymaggz on IG?" Toya asked, adding a waterfall curl to her client's hair.

"I think so. Lex just showed me her work."

"Girl, she's bomb as fuck! Plus, I love that she's confident in her own skin. She shows everyone that plus size is in too. I already know she'll have you lookin' amazin'."

Toya pulled the drape off of her client before the girl looked over her hair. She paid Toya before heading out the door. Toya grabbed another chair for me to put my feet up before I sat in her chair.

"What are we doing today?"

"A nice tight low ponytail with some curls in the ponytail."

"Low or high?"

"Low."

Toya and I made small talk as she styled my hair. Mid conversation, my phone vibrated. Reading the text from Kas, I twisted my face in confusion.

Kas: (11:27am) – *Did you get the delivery?*

Before I could respond, the bell over the door chimed

and in walked a guy holding a huge Edible Arrangement with *'I Love You'* balloons. I couldn't stop the tears that welled in my eyes. Although Kas and I had been on the outs, it warmed my heart to know he remembered my cravings.

"Is there a Mercedes here?" the delivery guy asked the receptionist.

"She's right here," Toya yelled. The guy walked over to me before handing me the vase filled with fruit, wrapped with the string of balloons. My mouth instantly watered at the sight of the pineapple. I always bragged about how fresh Edible Arrangements pineapples were.

The guy smiled before he turned to walk away. I pulled the card from the center.

Our lives are about to change forever

I'm indebted to you for the rest of my life for giving me three beautiful baby girls

Today is about YOU and you will be treated like the Queen you are

I love you until the end of time

-Kas

I immediately picked up my phone and dialed his number.

"I'm assuming you got it?" he answered.

"Yesss!" I sniffled. "Thank you so much."

"Don't start that crying. I had your car picked up."

"What do you mean you had my car picked up? How am I supposed to get around?"

"You'll be chauffeured. There's a driver outside in a Bentley for you."

Like a big ass baby, I immediately started crying again.

"You know you don't have to do this, right?"

"Yes, I do. We've been through a lot, most within the last few months. In the midst of it all, you may have forgotten that you're a beautiful black Queen and it's my job as your King to remind you of that," he said. "Wipe your face because I know you're ugly crying right now. I booked you a suite downtown at the Omni, as well, for you to get ready in. Your makeup lady will meet you there to do your face and your dress should be there already too. I'll see you at the shower and if you need anything between now and then, call me and I'll make it happen. Love you, Ma."

"Love you more," I said just above a whisper as the call disconnected. I stared at the bouquet of fruit in front of me and smiled as I plucked a piece off.

"I need me a nigga like him," Toya said reaching for fruit.

"Girl," I said shaking my head. Besides our recent hiccup, I had to admit that Kas was the perfect man. I know any female would have killed to have a man like him.

"He got a brother?"

"Yes and no," I answered.

"What the hell does that mean?"

"Yes, he does and no I can't put you on."

"Bitch you're a hater."

Toya and I laughed and made small talk as we fucked up the fruit from the arrangement and Toya finished my hair. Within an hour, I was done and heading outside. Just as he stated, a tinted out black Bentley truck was waiting for me with a driver leaning up against the car door.

"How are you today, Ms. Mercedes?"

"Large," I chuckled. "How are you?"

"Great! I'm Moises and I will be your designated driver today."

He opened the door and assisted me into the truck and then stuffed the balloons in with me.

"Any stops before going to the hotel?"

"No, my makeup appointment is in twenty minutes so we can head there."

I leaned back and closed my eyes and enjoyed the ride. It didn't take long to get to the hotel. Moises helped me out of the car and told me he would be back in three hours. I waddled to the front desk to get the key to my suite.

"Hi, I'm picking up the key to my suite. It should be under Mercedes Castro."

I didn't miss her look me up and down as if she was surprised, I was asking for a suite key before she started looking into her system.

"I'm sorry, I don't have a reservation under that name," she smirked.

"Try Kaseem Washington," I told her. She went back to typing on her computer before she began shaking her head.

"Nope, nothing under that name. You sure it's a suite?"

"Positive," I winked before pulling out my phone to call Kas. I put the phone on speaker as I dug deep for my wallet.

"What's up mama?" he answered.

"Hey, they're not finding a name under my name or yours. What did you book it under?"

"Mercedes Washington."

I looked over at the lady who flared her nostrils slightly as she typed in the name.

"I've located it. I just need your ID?"

I knew by now this bitch was just being difficult. I handed her my ID and leaned against the counter.

"Oh, I'm sorry. Because the name on the reservation doesn't match, I cannot give you the key. I'm sorry." I sighed and ran my tongue along my teeth as I shifted my weight from one foot to the other.

"I'm pullin' up outside," Kas said before the call disconnected.

"Why don't you grab your manager for me while we wait," I smiled. Her fake smile dropped at the mention of her manager. "Oh no honey, don't drop the smile now. Gon' head and smile as you march to get your manager."

Kas walked up to me just as I finished my statement.

"Let me get the key to my room I paid for," he told her before she walked away.

"C-can I have your name?"

"Kaseem Washington," he answered. "K-A-S-E-E-M."

She began searching the system and then grabbed keycards to program.

"Wait! So, you did all of this just to be extra? When I gave you his name, you told me you had no reservations under his name. Give me my damn key before I slap yo ass," I snapped. I didn't miss the scoff that escaped Kas' mouth as he slid the key off the counter and handed it to me. He planted a kiss on my cheek.

"Behave yourself."

"I always do unless bitches like her push my buttons. Was the makeup artist already here or do I have to go to her?"

"She should be up there. I got one key and gave it to her earlier, I left the other key at the desk for you but apparently, shortie had other plans."

"Shortie almost got fucked up."

"You need to hurry up and give birth," Kas laughed. "You're ruthless."

"Nah I'm nice, it's when people fuck with me for no reason that I get annoyed."

Kas chuckled again before kissing me and heading back out of the hotel. I rode up to the floor the suite was on and easily found the room. Walking inside, Margarita was all set up and waiting for me. I put my things down and she got right to work. We made small talk while she worked. Once she was done, I looked myself over in the mirror.

"Wow! This is amazing." The eye shadow matched spot on with my dress. "You did a bomb ass job. Now, this is my first-time wearing lashes. I can almost guarantee that by the end of the night they'll be rubbed off." We both shared as laugh as Margarita packed up her stuff. "I really appreciate it." I hugged her and walked her to the door. Once she left, I took a look at myself again in the mirror. I couldn't believe I was really about to be the mother of three. I could feel myself getting emotional, so I took a deep breath, patted my eyes and proceeded to get dressed. The shower was scheduled to start in about a half-hour and here I still sat in sweats.

My phone vibrated on the bed. Scooping it up, it was a number I didn't recognize. I almost ignored it until I remembered Moises said he was coming back.

"Hello?"

"Ms. Mercedes, I'm downstairs whenever you're ready," Moises stated.

"Okay, I'll be right down." I carefully pulled my dress on and eased it down over my bulging stomach. The way the dress hugged my stomach made it look perfectly round and made me feel even more beautiful. I couldn't help but pose in the mirror. I snapped a few pictures and sent some to Kas. I looked at my shoes and realized there was no way I was putting these on myself. I shot Kas a text letting him know I would need his help when I got to the venue. I grabbed the box of shoes, my wallet, and my keys and slid my feet into my slides before walking out the door. Walking through the lobby, I felt like all eyes were on me. As soon as I made it to the valet area, I saw the chick from the front desk. Part of me wanted to be petty but I had already taken my time getting dressed and I wasn't going to let her ruin my day. I winked at her before walking over to Moises, who was waiting for me at the truck. I was ready to celebrate my girls.

Chapter Eighteen

Kaseem

Cedes sent me a text letting me know she was pulling up. I met her at the car door and had to admit, my breath was taken away when I saw her. My lady looked absolutely gorgeous. She swung her feet out of the truck and handed me the box with her shoes. Pulling out her sandals, I helped her put them on before pulling her in for a deep kiss.

"You look amazing."

"Thank you," she blushed. I took her hand and helped her out of the car before allowing her to loop her arm in and walking her inside. Alexus, her mom, and my mom went all out with this Heaven-Sent theme. Every centerpiece was a cloud with three sleeping babies on a puff of cotton to make it look as if they were sleeping on clouds alongside random pictures, I found Mercedes most beautiful. The backdrop held the words "Heaven Sent" between two gold angel wings with curtains with different shades of pink behind it. I had to admit, I was impressed with the way it turned out.

"Where did you get these pictures?" she asked picking up the photo on the table closest to her. I knew she was going to ask that because through everything that we had been going through, Cedes had been staying at her mother's.

"I've got my ways. Plus, some you sent me."

"Why didn't you just have me do a maternity shoot?"

"I have one scheduled for you for next week, but I wanted you in rare form actually showing you."

She smiled as we walked around the hall greeting everyone and I didn't miss Cedes trying to make sure no embarrassing pictures.

"You can stop staring at the tables like that. I wouldn't embarrass you like that. I only picked ones where you are embracing pregnancy," I assured her. It was almost as if I could see her release the breath she was holding. It didn't take long before Lex spotted her and pulled her away from me. I watched in love as she interacted with everyone. All of her coworkers from work and family she hadn't spoken to in forever showed up.

"You good, bro?" Sha asked me wrapping his arm around my shoulder.

"Yeah man. I love the fact that Cedes is enjoying herself."

"Me too. How have y'all been?"

"I don't even know man. I do know that I'm getting out though."

"Outta what?"

"The game. I got one final run and then I'm done."

"Who's taking over?"

"Jay." I didn't miss the look of disappointment when I said it wasn't him. "Listen Sha, that shit that happened was too close to home. They're still gonna be watching. The first person they're gonna look at is you. We have plenty of legal businesses, take one of those. You'll still be well off," I explained.

"You're right." I knew it wasn't what Sha wanted to hear but it was what it was. "Can I ride with you at least?"

I cut my eyes at him.

"I'll let you know."

Just as we had finished our conversation, Cedes came over and grabbed my hand and pulled me around the venue with her. The turnout was great, and it felt great watching the smile on Cedes face all night long.

*****

Two Weeks Later…

I stepped into my walk-in closet to grab my sweatsuit as Cedes sat on the bed, folding the girl's clothes she had just washed. I pulled my sweats up as I walked out of the closet.

"Are you sure about this?" she asked. She began rubbing her stomach as she sat back. "I'm not getting a good feeling about this."

"You okay?" I asked her ignoring her question.

"Yeah, just some Braxton Hicks. Don't ignore me though."

"Ma, I'll be good. I'm not doing anything but riding and watching," I told her.

"Okay," she said sighing deeply.

"Call Lex to come sit with you." I looked at the time and saw it was going on six. "I should be back by midnight the very latest." The look of worry never left Cedes' face.

"Can you share your location with me?" she asked. I grabbed my phone and turned on my location so she would know my whereabouts at all times. I finished getting dressed as she called Lex to come sit with her. Just as I stomped my foot into my mid-top black AF1s, Jay pulled up. I pulled my hoodie over my head before placing a kiss on Cedes' lips.

"I'll make sure to keep checking in with you. I'll let you know when we get there and when we are leaving to come back."

"Okay."

"I love you."

"I love you more," she said as I walked out of the bedroom. I jogged down the stairs and out the door to Jay's car. I said a quick prayer that everything went straight.

"What's good, boy?" I dapped Jay up.

"Shit man. Is Julio's girl meeting us there?"

"Yeah, Julio said she flew into Boston and was meeting us there."

"A'ight let's get going."

Jay turned up the music before jumping on 95N. We didn't speak the entire ride. I used the time to reflect on life outside of the game. After this, I was going to be a legitimate businessman. No more having to worry about the boys in blue. No more unnecessary out of town trips. All my money was mainly legit. I would still help Jay clean his shit through one of the businesses he ran, but other than that, I would be clean.

Before I knew it, we were getting off the exit to the crib we were meeting ole boy at. Check under that seat," Jay said. "Grab that burner... just in case."

Nothing more needed to be said. I grabbed it and checked it to make sure it was loaded, and the safety was on. You could never be too careful in this business. I trusted this Nicki chick to an extent and that was only because she was Julio's lady, but that doesn't mean my guard was down.

Within fifteen minutes, we were pulling up to the address Julio gave. As we climbed out of the car, a heavily tinted vehicle drove by. I followed it with my eyes until the taillights were no longer visible to me. Walking across the street, the front door opened, and Nicki stood there.

"Welcome gentlemen," she greeted. She stood to the side allowing me and Jay to walk in. "Jerry is waiting for you at the kitchen." I shoved my hands in the front part of my hoodie, gripping the handle of the piece that was in the waistband of my sweats.

"What's good?" the guy I assumed was Jerry stated. "I'm Jerry. Why don't y'all have a seat?"

I looked at Jay who spoke before I could.

"Nah, I prefer to stand. I'm Jay though and this is Kas."

Nicki stood off to the side of the kitchen. The vibe I was getting was starting to feel off, so I definitely wanted this shit to be over. I shifted my weight from one foot to the other.

"You nervous my man?" Jerry asked. "I offered you a seat and you prefer to stand but you look uncomfortable standing."

"Nah I'm good. This meeting should be quick. Did Nicki give you the rundown?"

"Nah, she said that's what y'all were coming to do," he snapped.

"Aye man, all of that is not necessary. Let's get down to business," Jay stepped in. "How long you been in the game?"

"Long enough."

"Listen Jerry, let's make this business shit easy," I said. "We do the same shit you do, so let's get on the same damn page."

He sat back and interlocked his fingers.

"I've been in the game about four years," he answered. "I've been waiting to be put on to a larger scale, so when my cousin Nicki here said her nigga was that nigga, I just had to get down. I'll be honest, I was expecting to meet him, but he always sends someone else to handle business.

He says I'm supposed to be working with y'all."

"Yeah, I run some shit down in Rhode Island and we've been expanding out here. You know where all your spots are gonna be?" Jay asked.

"Yeah, they're all set and my young boys are in place."

"Are these men you can trust?"

"With my life."

I nodded as I listened to Jay finish schooling this dude. I took the chance to read him and feel him out. So far, I wasn't trusting him, and I would definitely let Julio know he needed a new dude.

"You'll get a call a week before drops are made to let you know when and which spot it'll be dropped at. Make sure you have the set niggas to always do your breakdowns. I'll be riding up here every two weeks to pick up the money, so definitely make sure they're always on point. That's the one thing big man does not like, his money being short. We can make this business relationship one of the smoothest. Always use burners whenever making business calls and change it up often. Here's my number." Jay slid a faulty business card across the table. Jerry picked up the card and looked at it before nodding. "Welcome to the team my nigga," Jay said extending his hand. "Let's get this money."

We both dapped each other up.

"The first drop will be here tomorrow, and it'll already be broken down. My young bull Tony will drop it to each spot by six in the morning, so make sure your men are ready. It's early in the month and it's tax time, so y'all should be booming. Remind them not to draw any unwanted attention to these spots. They were selected specifically by the big man and he hates the attention of the boys in blue," Jay reminded.

"I got it."

"I'll be back in a few days to check on shit and meet your guys. If you need me before then, just holla at me."

We dapped him up again, said bye to Nicki and backed out of the crib. One thing we never did was turn our backs to a nigga we didn't know. Once we got outside, we headed towards the car.

"Jay, be easy with that nigga. I'm not feelin' his vibe," I told him.

"Yo," we heard, as we were halfway across the street. Turning around, Jerry stepped out of the house and raised his arm. Before either of us could react…

Pop!

Pop!

Pop!

Pop!

I couldn't even reach for my piece before the hot led filled my chest, arm, and torso. I could hear the bullets flying again but each time I tried to speak, I began choking. I tried to keep my eyes open, but they were becoming heavier and heavier. Eventually, the gunfire stopped.

"Kas!" I could hear Jay calling my name. I tried to answer but I couldn't respond. "Kas stay with me, my nigga." I kept trying to speak.

"Kids..." I gasped. "Cedes."

"You're not leaving them, Kas. Stay with me, nigga. I'ma get you some help. Keep your eyes open."

I could hear sirens, but they sounded so far away. I could feel Jay pressing on my chest, but I was slowly losing it.

"Stay with me, Kas!" Jay yelled. I could hear other voices, but everything was getting dark. Jay's voice was getting further and further away. It wasn't long before it all went black.

Chapter Nineteen

Mercedes

My Braxton Hicks weren't letting up and I was starting to feel as if they were the real thing. I kept checking my phone waiting for Kas to check in with me. The more I worried, the more the girls moved and the more my contractions came on. I was breathing through them as best as I could, but they were coming on harder.

The doorbell rang. Looking at my phone, I checked the app for the cameras and saw Lex standing there. I rubbed my stomach as I made it to the door. Opening it, the pain was clearly etched on my face.

"Are you okay?" Alexus asked.

"My contractions are literally hitting back to back and I can't shake this bad feeling about Kas," I admitted.

"Oh no, don't start that he's doing wrong shit, Cedes," Lex said as she grabbed my arm. "He's been on the straight and narrow as you've told me."

"Shut up, Lex," I said. "Come inside."

I moved to the side while still breathing through the major and minor contractions.

"What's going on with Kas now?" Lex asked closing the door behind her and heading to the living room.

"Kas and Jay made this run to meet the people who I'm guessing are going to be helping Jay with this expansion into Boston. He was supposed to let me know when he got there and when he was coming back, but it's been a few hours and I haven't heard anything. My texts aren't even going through as iMessages, only text messages, meaning his phone is off. This ain't like Kas at all," I began to cry.

"No! Nope, we're not going to think the worse. Have you called Jay? I'm sure they're fine."

"No, I haven't checked with him. Let me try."

Before I could even call Jay, I felt this odd pop inside my stomach.

"Oh shit," I said. "I think my water broke."

"What? Oh, God. Okay, let's stand up."

Lex immediately began panicking and pacing.

"Alexus relax! Shit, you would think you're the one that's pregnant. The contractions are spreading apart, but I definitely gotta go in," I told her. The moment I stood up the water gushed out.

"Are you sure you're not peeing yourself?" Lex asked.

"Go away!" I chuckled. I gripped the arm of the couch as another contraction hit me. I was able to breathe through it. "I'm gonna take a quick shower. Can you grab the suitcase by the closet door and the diaper bag off the bed?"

"Shower? Shouldn't we be rushing to the hospital?"

"Go do what I said, you damn worrywart. Shit! I need a clean cat when I'm in delivery."

"Bitch, you're crazy! Just a damn minute ago you were barely able to stand and open the door, now your ass wanna take showers and your water has already broken. Damn. Something is wrong with your ass," Lex complained. I shook my head and headed to the bathroom. The contractions seemed to have calmed, but they were definitely strong. I made the shower quick as I could and went into my room to grab some sweats.

"I tried to call both Kas and Jay, but I got no answer," Lex revealed. Something was wrong. I could feel it.

"Can you call my OB?"

"What's her number under?"

"OBGYN," I told her. "They're gonna page her most likely."

I grabbed socks and put them on my feet as Lex gave the person on the other end of info. I couldn't help but wonder about Kas. I hoped his phone died but he was on his way. Just as Lex hung up the phone, I slid my feet into my slides.

"Let's go," I said shutting off the lights and leaving the house. Lex drove as I sat in the passenger's side calling and texting Kas while breathing through contractions. It took us no time to get to Women and Infants. While I was checking in, contractions were coming back to back. It took no time for them to get me into a labor and delivery room and a doctor to get in to assess the situation. They hooked up multiple heart monitors and a contraction machine to monitor the babies. Despite all of the pain, I was only dilated to two centimeters. They confirmed my water did indeed break and wanted to monitor to see if I would progress. I continued to call Kas and Jay and got nothing.

"Cedes, try and get some rest. I'm sure we'll be here for a while," Lex said. "I called mom, dad and Kas' mom. I asked Kas' mom if she heard from Kas, Sha or Jay, but she said she hasn't heard from either."

My phone vibrated in my hand just before Lex could say anything else. I didn't recognize the number but saw it was a Mass number.

"Hello," I answered immediately.

"Hi, I'm looking for a Mercedes Castro," a woman said. Immediately, I could feel my heart racing.

"T-this is she," I stuttered. "Who is this?"

"My name is Camille. I'm a nurse at Boston Medical Center. I have a Kaseem Washington here and was told to call you."

"W-what happened to Kaseem?" I screamed.

"Are you able to come down to the hospital?"

"No! I'm in labor! What the fuck happened?"

"Cedes, calm down!" Lex said. "Give me the phone." She snatched the phone before I could say anything else. The monitor attached to me started going crazy and a team of doctors rushed in as Lex stepped out. Following the last doctor was my mother rushing inside to see what was happening.

"Ms. Castro, I need you to calm down. Your heart rate is elevated, your blood pressure is going up and you're putting the babies in distress," Dr. Hardaway said.

"Mom, go find Lex and find out what is going on with Kaseem and Jay! A nurse was calling to tell me something before she snatched the phone," I cried. "I need to know what is going on!"

"No. Ms. Castro," Dr. Hardaway called out to me. "I need you to focus on these babies! Their lives rely on you."

Lex peeked into the room and called for my mom to come out. I didn't miss the tears in her eyes and immediately burst into tears. The pain I felt in my chest had me howling like a wolf to the moon.

"Alright, these babies are in distress, we're doing an emergency C-section," I heard Dr. Hardaway say. It only made me cry harder because it had always been a goal of mine to have a natural delivery. My mother returned with a look of worry over her face.

"What is going on?" I cried.

"Nothing for you to worry about, love. I'm right here to help you get through this C-section. Worry about everything else later. Right now, we gotta get these babies here," she said. I wasn't buying her shit. Something was wrong with Kas and Jay and I was tired of being kept in the dark.

Before I knew it, they were prepped and ready to begin the process. My mind was on what could be going on with Kas. My thoughts were interrupted by the most beautiful sound I have ever heard.

"Baby A is here," Dr. Hardaway shouted. To hear my daughter my daughter's cry was a dream come true. I had prayed for years for a healthy baby and so far, I had one. It wasn't long before another bellowing cry followed. "There's baby B!"

"Oh my God," my mother said. The tears were falling freely from her eyes. "Cedes, they are gorgeous." I could hear my girls whimpering as I saw nurses over both beds.

"Here's baby C," Dr. Hardaway called. Only she wasn't crying.

"Mom, what's wrong with my baby?" I asked. It felt like forever and I was worried that something was wrong.

"They're suctioning out her mouth and nose," she said never breaking her eye contact with the doctors and nurses on the other side of the curtain.

"Mom," I called just above a whisper. Before she could look at me, I heard my baby girl cough and begin to whimper. I released the breath I had no idea I was holding. My mom left my side and went to see the babies. I laid there as tears fell from my eyes overwhelmed with emotion. My girls were here, but Kas was not. The worse part about Kas not being here was I didn't know where he was, what happened, and most of all, if he was even alive.

Chapter Twenty

Alexus

I paced the floor of the waiting room. My mind was racing a mile a minute. I was not prepared for what the nurse said when I took the phone from Cedes. I sat in the chair and thought back again over the conversation.

"Hello," I spoke into the phone.

"Hello?"

"Hi, I'm Alexus, Mercedes' sister. I'm not sure what's going on. She's in labor right now ready to give birth to triplets and she's super stressed as it is. What is going on?"

"I'm sorry. My name is Camille and I'm a nurse at

BMC. This probably isn't the best time, but Mr. Washington was rushed in with at least three gunshot wounds."

The air was knocked out of me. I felt like I couldn't breathe.

"I-is he okay?"

"He's in surgery right now, but to be honest, I have no idea. One was to the chest."

"Was anybody with him?" I asked.

"There was a guy who came in with him, he gave me this number and told me to call a Mercedes Castro and tell her what was going on and then he left. He didn't say his name though," Camille said.

That must've been Jay, I thought to myself.

"Listen," she continued. *"I don't even know if I'm supposed to do this, but I'll do my best to keep you updated."*

"Please do."

"I hope Mercedes has a safe delivery," Camille said before she hung up. I threw myself into the chair and tried to gather my thoughts. Going through Cedes' phone, I located Sha's number and tried to call him, but got nothing. I tried Jay's number again and was surprised it rang.

"Cedes?" he answered.

160

"*No! Her sister, Alexus. Jay, what the fuck is going on?*" *I asked.*

"*Shit's bad man. All bad! Everything was smooth until we left the crib. Fuck man! I can't talk right now.*"

"*Jay! Don't you hang up on me! Mercedes is in labor and about to give birth. She's freakin' the fuck out,*" *I exclaimed.*

"*Lex, I can't say much and you know that,*" *he said letting me know it wasn't legal shit and he couldn't say it over the phone.* "*My nigga flat-lined on his way to the hospital. They were able to revive him, but last I knew he was in surgery. I paid this lil' nurse there to call Cedes and let her know and keep me updated cuz I had to go back. This shit wasn't supposed to go down. I wanna come back and fill y'all in, but I can't leave my nigga here alone.*" *Jay sounded more than he rambling.*

"*What do I tell Cedes?*"

"*The truth.*"

"*She's just given birth, Jay!*"

"*I know that, but she needs to know. Fuck man! I shoulda told his ass to stay home. Fuck! Fuck! Fuck!*" *I stayed silent as Jay ranted on.* "*How are the babies?*" *he stopped and asked.*

"*I don't know. I stepped out when the nurse called. My*

mom was with her," I told him.

"Go check on your sister. I'll be back in town in a few hours and I'll come see y'all."

Jay didn't allow me to respond before he hung up.

The elevator dinging brought me out of my thoughts. Looking up, I saw my mother coming out.

"How is she?" I asked her.

"The babies are here," she revealed. My hands shot over my mouth.

"That fast?"

"She had to have an emergency C-section. Baby Kassie's heart rate was dropping and Cedes pressure was rising. Kassie wasn't crying when she came out. It seems she began to poop and swallowed some, so they are suctioning her more frequently. The good thing is they are all breathing on their own. Dr. Hardaway is actually surprised as to how good they're doing at less than thirty-six weeks. They're definitely fighters."

"How much did they weigh?"

"Kashmere is four pounds even, Kassidy is four pounds two ounces and Kassandra is four pounds five ounces. They are going to be monitored for a few hours especially Kassie," my mom said. "Cedes is being moved to recovery. What's going on with Kaseem?"

I sighed. "He got shot."

"He got what? What the fuck happened?"

"I don't know. Jay didn't say much."

My mother sat down and threw her head into her hands.

"This shit is bad. All bad. Have you called his mother?"

"Ma, I don't know what to do honestly. I don't wanna tell Cedes, but then again, she deserves to know. From what Jay told me, Kas flat-lined but was revived. He and the nurse said he was in surgery, but it was touch and go."

"Shit! Cedes is going to lose her mind. I gotta call Justine too." My mother got up and walked away. On one hand, I was excited for my sister, but on the other hand, my heart broke for her. April 4th was forever going to be the date that my sister's life changed.

Chapter Twenty One

Jay

After hanging up with Alexus, I focused back on the road. I was fucked up. I felt like I failed my nigga. Kas was just tellin' me about this nigga and he tried to take us the fuck out. Thinking about it caused me to grip the steering wheel tighter. As I pulled into the neighborhood, I could still see cops blocking off the street. I thought I saw the nigga drop on the porch, but I didn't know if he was dead.

I grabbed a pack of wet wipes from the glove box to clean my hands and zipped my hoodie to cover my blood-soaked shirt. I parked at the end of the street, pulled the hood over my head and walked down the block. I squeezed through until I got close to the crime tape.

"What happened?" I asked a lady who was standing there.

"Someone got shot in the street and apparently the one on the porch is dead."

Good! I thought to myself. I wish it was me who bodied the muthafucka but whoever did, I owe them.

"It was just those two?" I asked.

"Those two were the only ones hit. The one who got shot in the street was taken away by ambulance, but I overheard them say this dude was DOA," she said. I heard all I needed to hear. Jerry was dead. My only concern now was where the fuck Nicki's ass was. I pulled out my burner and shot a *911* text to Julio. There's no way Nicki's ass was innocent. I walked away from the crowd and back to my car. I jumped back on the highway. I pulled my phone and called Cedes number back. I didn't even realize I didn't have the nurse's number to check on Kas myself.

"Hello?" her sister answered.

"Aye, let me get the number that nurse called you from." The phone got silent before I felt it vibrate.

"I just text it to you," she said.

"Bet."

166

I tapped her number in the message and listened to it ring. It rolled over to voicemail, so I hung up and called again. Shortie ignored the call. Before I could call again, a text came in.

508-471-9912 (1:57am) – Who is this?

Me (1:58am) – I'm checkin' on my nigga who I came in with earlier. What's the word?

I took the exit to 95 heading back to the city. I knew there was nothing I could do tonight for Kas, and I much rather would get back and fill everyone in. Normally I would blast music, but right now, I needed to be in my thoughts. My phone alerted me of a message that Julio would be in town by morning. A second message followed.

508-471-9912 (2:05am) – He's out of surgery. The next twenty-four hours will be touch and go. The one in the chest missed his heart my mere inches and the one in the torso nicked his left lung and grazed the pulmonary artery. They were able to stop the internal bleeding but placed him in a medical coma to allow his body to heal. He has a long road ahead and if he makes the next 24hrs, he'll be fine. He's lucky.

I took a deep breath. I had faith my nigga would be good.

Me (2:08am) – You think they would transfer him to

where he's from?

I knew Cedes would wanna be by his side, but with just having the babies, she could not stretch herself that damn thin being between BMC and the hospital. With just having the girls, I knew she was not gonna make that trip with the girls daily. I needed to get my nigga home ASAP.

508-471-9912 (2:10am) *– it would depend on where he's going and if they are able to treat him. You would have to talk to the doctors about it. Typically, parents or their spouse makes the decision.*

Me (2:11am) *– Bet. Keep me updated.*

I would let Mama Justine know she needed to get him moved. Once I entered into Pawtucket, I called Alexus to see where she was. She told me that she and her mom had just got to her mom's house since Cedes was finally moved into recovery. She told me Kas' mom was on her way there. I realized I hadn't spoken to Sha. After hanging up with Lex, I called Sha.

"What's good?" he answered on the second ring sounding like he was wide-awake.

"Where you at?"

"I just got a call from moms to meet her at Cedes mom's crib, so I'm heading there."

"A'ight. I'm heading there myself."

"Bet," he said as he disconnected. It didn't take me long to get to Cedes' mom's spot. With the amount of cars outside, you would think it was the middle of the afternoon rather than the middle of the night. I took another deep breath before killing the engine and heading inside. I knew everyone would have questions and I just hoped I had all of the answers.

Before I could knock on the door, Sha opened the door and pushed me backwards.

"What the hell you doing?" I asked him.

"I gotta holla at you," he said. He looked back at the door before walking down the stairs.

"Can it wait? Everyone's been on pins and needles waiting for me to get here and tell them what happened."

"Nah, I gotta tell you now." I jogged down the steps behind him.

"What's up?"

"I bodied that nigga," he spat.

"Huh?"

"Kas told me all about the run y'all was makin' but wouldn't let me ride. You know me, I always got my brother's back. I followed y'all out there and when I saw that nigga shoot at y'all, I popped his ass. To watch my brother, drop the way he did, I felt like my heart shattered. I made sure that bitch was gone. I had to get outta there once I heard the boys coming," he explained.

"What the fuck, Sha. Where's the piece?"

"I tossed that shit."

"Your prints?"

"Had on gloves."

I felt uneasy that Sha got rid of the gun because I wasn't 100% sure it couldn't be traced back to him.

"How's Kas?" he asked. I sighed and relayed the messages I exchanged with the nurse from BMC.

"The bad thing is, Cedes fuckin' gave birth."

"Get the fuck outta here!"

"The nurse called her to tell her as she was in labor. Let me go in here so I can fill them in," I said heading towards the house. "Keep that shit you told me to yourself too."

He nodded as we headed inside to break the news to the family. This was the last thing I ever wanted to do, but I knew shit like this came with the game. I just never thought it would happen to Kas or myself.

*****

Six Hours Later...

I stared at the ceiling as I heard my phone ring. I had laid here for three hours trying to sleep, but I couldn't get the picture of my nigga out of my mind. Every time I closed my eyes, I saw my nigga choking on blood. It was like a nightmare that wouldn't stop.

I let the phone roll over to voicemail. It wasn't long before it rang again. Sighing, I grabbed my phone off the nightstand and saw it was Julio.

"Yo," I answered.

"My house, thirty minutes," he said before hanging up. I dropped the phone on my bed. I threw my head in my hands as my phone chimed, alerting me of a text. Looking at the phone, I saw it was the nurse from BMC. I quickly unlocked it and read the text.

508-471-9912 (8:24am) – I'm leaving work but will be returning early afternoon because I'm working a double. So far, his vitals have been stable, but the coma is helping that. I have a friend who is working this upcoming shift so I'll check in with her and keep you updated.

Me (8:25am) – Appreciate it

I hopped up to take a quick shower before heading to Julio's. I could not wait for this shit to be over and my nigga to bounce back. I didn't know these Boston niggas and if they were all like Jerry, I wanted no business with them and if Julio was smart, he would leave that shit be. Them niggas moved like snakes and I would hate to have to body them all just to make a point.

I pulled up to Julio's crib with two minutes to spare. Before I could even close the door to the car, Julio's bodyguard had the door open.

"What's good?" I greeted him. He simply nodded before closing the door and leading me to Julio's office. I was surprised to enter and see Nicki standing there. This was one time I was pissed I was not packing coming into Julio's crib. I ran my tongue across my teeth as I glared in her direction.

"What's going on?" Julio asked as I'm sure my face spoke a thousand words.

"Why don't you ask Nicki here?"

"I'm asking you."

"She set us up," I blurted. Nicki's eyes shot wide open as if I revealed her deepest darkest secrets.

"Do explain," Julio said sitting up and leaning forward towards his desk.

"This nigga you had us meet was this bitch's cousin. Off rip, the nigga had a nasty ass attitude. We handled what we had to handled, and we leave. We didn't even make it to the car before this nigga comes outside blazing. My fuckin' right hand is laid up in the hospital fighting for his life behind this bitch and she has the nerve to be standing here like all is fuckin' well," I snapped.

"I have no idea what you're talking about," she said nonchalantly. Before I even realized, I lunged towards her but was caught quickly by Julio's bodyguards.

"Lie again bitch! Lie the fuck again and I swear to God I will have your parents searching the Providence River for your fuckin' body parts. The least you can do is be fuckin' real. Do you know my nigga missed the birth of his only three kids he will ever fuckin' have? Do you know I had to tell his entire fuckin' family he may not ever get to meet his kids? As he was fightin' for his life, his wife was givin' life to his kids! Don't you have a son? How the fuck would you feel? All this for fuckin' what? Bitch, you're fuckin' the plug! I can tell just by the way your 'cousin' was talkin' that he was a greedy muthafucka and you probably are the same way. Is he even really your cousin?" I couldn't stop spewing off questions and statements. "If I had to bet every dollar I owned, he's probably a nigga you fuckin'."

"Alright enough," Julio interjected. "Nicki, step out." I kept my eyes on her as she walked out. As the door closed behind her, I put my attention back on Julio. "How's Kaseem?"

I sighed as I finally sat down across from him. "He's fighting. They have him in a coma as he heals internally." I told him what the nurse had relayed to me. "He's almost in the clear."

"His wife gave birth?" I nodded.

"I don't know if his family told her. I do know when she finds out, she's going to lose it. It's just all fucked up, man."

"Listen, let me apologize Jay. If I know my men, Nicki is dead already. My product was removed from all of the Boston spots; I'm all set with them. It's evident that they like messy shit and you know I don't do messy. If it ain't broke, don't fix it. Rhode Island makes me good money, as do my boys in New York and Jersey. I'll retry Mass with my own team of guys, but I don't want you to worry about that. Handle your business and keep me updated on Kas. I'll be sending something to Kas' wife as well."

I nodded. For the first time in the last twelve hours, I felt like I could relax.

"You look like you got the world on your shoulders," Julio said.

"I feel like it. I haven't slept worth a damn. It's fuckin' me up that Kas is in the hospital fighting for his life. It's makin' it worse that his wife had to give birth without him, and she doesn't even know if he'll make it home. I feel like I'm to blame because knowing she could technically go at any moment, I shoulda told his ass to stay home," I answered honestly.

"Nah, I'll take the blame. Kas said he wanted out, but I was adamant about the final run. It's something I'll take on the chin and own up to. Keep me updated on him and his kids. Let his wife know if she needs anything, don't hesitate to call."

"Bet."

I dapped up Julio before being guided out. Checking my phone, I saw Cedes had called me. I didn't know if it was her or her sister, but I was dreading speaking to Cedes. Eventually, I knew that I would have to man up and answer any questions she has. Calling Cedes back, my heart sank hearing her voice.

"Jay," she said just above a whisper. "Where is he?"

"BMC," I responded.

"What happened?"

I sighed. "I'll be up there to talk to you in person. What's your room number?"

She gave me her room number and I told her I was on my way. I mentally had to prepare myself for one of the most difficult conversations I would have to have.

Chapter Twenty Two

Mercedes

I held Kashmere and Kassidy, staring between the two of them as I waited for Jay to show up. My emotions were a hot ass mess. It was so hard to enjoy the birth of my girls knowing Kas was laid up in the hospital. Alexus gave me the short version, but I needed to know everything.

I had to admit, Kashmere looked like a spitting image of Kas. Kassidy had my slanted eyes and pouty mouth, yet Kas' nose. I spent a little bit of time with Kassandra in the NICU as they monitored her breathing. The little bit of meconium that she swallowed did a number because she still had that shit in her lungs…literally.

My mind kept drifting to Kaseem. Lex had told me what happened, but I needed to hear it firsthand. Just as I laid Lil' Kas back in her bassinet, a light knock came to the door.

"Come in," I called. Jay walked in looking like he had the weight of the world on his shoulders.

"Hey sis," he offered me a half-smile. "Congratulations."

"Thank you," I said as he leaned in to give me a kiss on the cheek. "How are you and don't lie?"

"Honestly, horrible. It's like a nightmare I can't wake up from. I'm filled with nothing but guilt because my nigga shoulda been by your side. You gave birth without your man because of me. I don't know if I'll ever forgive myself for that shit."

"Jay, it's not your fault. Neither of you knew this would happen. I hate that it happened, but let's be glad he's still alive." Jay nodded and I saw him look in Kassidy's bassinet. "Go ahead and pick her up."

He looked at me before going and washing his hands and gabbed Kassidy out of her bassinet before taking a seat.

"Tell me what happened," I said to him. He took a deep breath before he started the story. The entire time he spoke, his eyes never left Kassidy's face. I watched as a lone tear roll down his cheek. He took another deep breath as he finished talking.

"How's he doing now?" I asked.

"I haven't checked in with the nurse in a few hours, but she's goin' back to work soon and she'll give me an update. I'm tryna talk Justine into getting him transferred down here. At least then you'll be able to see him."

"Yeah, something is gonna have to shake."

Jay and I talked for another hour and a half as he bonded with the girls. While talking to Jay, the nurse from BMC shot him a text letting him know Kas' vitals were remaining stable. It gave me some relief knowing he was still fighting.

Just as Jay was leaving, Justine walked in. She kissed his cheek and told him to hold off on leaving. Jay leaned against the wall as Justine kissed both babies and washed her hands.

"I contacted BMC this morning. They want to watch him for another day or so to make sure he remains stable, but then they will transfer him down here. They are gonna talk to some doctors here to make sure they are ready for him," she said. I breathed a sigh of relief at the thought he would be closer to home. "How long are you gonna be here, Cedes?"

"Another four damn days. I'm hoping by then, Kassandra's infection clears up and she can go home. They say it's slowly coming up and out," I explained. "I have no idea how I'm going to do it with three damn babies and trying to heal from a C-section."

"Mercedes, you have help! Don't be afraid to ask for it. It's one thing healing from a C-section with one baby, but with three, you *will* need help. Plus, I know once Kaseem is transferred here, you'll really stretch yourself out trying to be here for him. What I need you to remember is you can't be there for anybody else until you take care of yourself. These three little ladies now rely on you, Cedes. Take care of you so you can take care of them," Justine explained. I knew exactly what she was saying, and she was right. I fought so hard to have these babies and I needed to be there for them.

"I hear you," I told her.

"I mean it, Mercedes. If you need anything, do not hesitate to pick up the phone," Justine reiterated.

"Same. I don't know shit about caring for a baby, but I'll do whatever I can to be there," Jay stated. I knew they meant it.

"I'm gonna take this time to find me as well. I don't want to be in the place where Kas and I were right before this shit happened. I want us to go back to how we were when nothing or nobody else mattered but us."

"Only you can fix that, Mercedes. You now have three new meanings at life and love. Be the woman you want these girls to be. Show and give the love you want them to show and give to the world. You do that and you'll be perfectly fine. I have no doubt about it," Justine stated.

For the next few hours, we all sat around and talked. It felt good to relax. Between Kassandra fighting off her infection and Kas fighting for his life, I wouldn't feel complete until both of them were home and our family was together.

Chapter Twenty Three

Kaseem

I couldn't believe this shit. I didn't know if I was more pissed at the fact I got shot or that I missed the birth of my kids. That's something I would probably never forgive myself for missing. Looking at the pictures Cedes showed me and seeing them on FaceTime had me wanting to run to them. It bugged the fuck outta me to watch Cedes walk out the door and me being stuck here in the hospital.

I sighed heavily and thought back to the day I was shot. I should have gone with my gut instinct and left the moment the nigga opened his mouth. The one time I ignored my gut almost cost me my life. I wanted that nigga dead.

My thoughts were interrupted by a light knock on the door. Turning, I spotted Jay walking in.

"Oh shit! When did you wake up?" he asked me rushing to my side and dapping me up. I grimaced in pain but was glad to see my nigga.

"Maybe about an hour or so. I was kickin' it with Cedes and finally got to see my girls."

"She brought them up here?"

"No, she showed me some pics and my mom happened to call while she was here, so I saw them on FaceTime," I explained.

"How does it feel, man?"

"I don't even know how to explain it. My heart just feels whole and I feel like I have a whole new outlook on life, or maybe it's because I got shot."

"Maybe it's both."

"Aye man," I said getting a little serious. "I wanna thank you for being there with me that night. You stayed by my side and probably saved my life. For that, I appreciate you for life."

"That goes without saying Kas. You went out there with me and for me. I would be a Goddamn fool to leave you in your time of need. You're my brother and family doesn't leave behind family. However, you need to be thankin' your brother."

"Did I not just thank you?" I joked.

"Shaheem."

"Shaheem?" I repeated.

Jay looked towards the door to make sure it was closed and nobody else was there.

"Why would I be thankin' Shaheem?"

"Shaheem's the one who bodied that nigga."

"Get the fuck outta here," I said. There was no way I wasn't believing that shit.

"Nigga, believe me, it wasn't me who bodied him although I wish it was. I ducked then went back to find you. The bullets stopped flying and that nigga was down. I never had a chance to fire back."

"How the fuck would Shaheem get there?"

"He told me he asked you to ride but you told him no. He followed anyway in his own whip."

I thought back on the heavily tinted car that rode by as we crossed the street. My brother had to have been behind the wheel. I had to admit, I owed my little brother my fuckin' life. I had always been the one wanting to protect him but when it absolutely mattered the most, he protected me as best as he could.

"Damn," I said.

"I felt the same way when he told me. The problem is, he tossed the piece and I don't know where. I just hope wherever he tossed it, it doesn't get linked back to him," Jay explained.

"He'll be good. Might've been a dumb move but he'll be good."

"I'm glad you're good though," Jay said dapping me up again. "I thought I lost you, my nigga."

"You know I don't go out easy. Have you talked to Julio?" I asked.

"BRUH! He came and met me, and Nicki's ass was with him and tried to act like she had nothing going on and she had no idea it was gonna happen. I literally tried to jump the table on her ass," he said.

I couldn't help but laugh at the picture of Jay's big ass tryna jump across the table at someone. I held my chest in discomfort.

"Stop makin' me laugh, bitch," I chuckled.

"Anyway, Julio handled her and said he got you and Cedes for whatever. He's shutting down the traps in Boston and had his shit taken back."

"Damn, Boston woulda made him some good money too," I said.

"Yeah, but until he can get his own team there, he's all set."

I nodded in understanding. Jay and I chopped it up about random shit. The nurses and doctors kept coming in and out checking on me. My moms came rushing into the room.

"Oh my God! Thank you, Jesus! My baby is awake. I have been waiting for this for weeks. My God I thought I lost you. Thank you, Jesus," she had my head smashed into her chest.

"I won't be awake if you don't let me breathe," I muffled. She pulled my head away and started planting kisses all over my face. "Moms, chill. I'm good."

"Listen boy, I thought I lost your big-headed ass so let me get my love in. Have they said anything about when you'll be able to go home?"

"They just said they want to make sure my vitals stay stable for a few days on its own. Honestly though, I'm tryna go home like yesterday. I need to meet my kids and be around my lady. Y'all have helped her tremendously while I've been down but it's time for me to be the father to my kids and the husband my lady needs me to be," I said.

"You gotta get back to 100% yourself, Kaseem. You're no good to them if you cannot take care of you. It wouldn't be fair to Cedes to have her take care of you and take care of the three babies."

"I hear you. Laying here is only gonna piss me off even more. I'll always take care of me, but I'm gonna do all I can to take care of the kids I created regardless of the pain. From what they've told me, I've been knocked out for weeks, I've rested enough." My mother knew she was losing this battle. I knew I would experience pain for a while, but I would fight through it. Cedes and my girls need me too.

*****

Three Days Later...

"Alright Mr. Washington, you're all set," the nurse stated as she handed me my discharge papers. "Your scripts have already been sent to the pharmacy and should be ready within an hour. If you have any side effects from the medication, come back and see us as soon as possible. Do you have any questions?"

"Nah, I'm good. Thank you."

She smiled and walked out. She had brought me a wheelchair, but I wasn't being pushed out in that shit. I told her I was good and walked out to the front wraparound of the hospital to where Jay was waiting for me. I was glad to be outta this bitch. I needed a home-cooked meal and I couldn't wait to start bonding with my babies.

"Appreciate you scoopin' me, homie," I said closing the door behind me. He headed off in the direction of my house.

"No need to thank me, nigga. Now that you're good, I can get back to the money. I'll run the legit shit until you're ready. You're done with this street shit whether you wanna be or not."

"Nigga, who you? My daddy?" I joked.

"Hell naw. You gettin' shot was too close to the streets takin' you out. You got a new reason to live; three of 'em to be exact. Leave the street shit to me. The same shit you preached to Sha, take heed to yourself."

I stared out the window as I let what Jay say sink in. I was done with the street shit, but I knew I would miss the thrill of it eventually.

"I gotta handle one more thing though," I said.

"Nah Kas. You ain't handling shit. Let it go. The nigga who tried to take you out is dead. What the fuck else you gotta handle?"

"Shanie. I ain't forget she tried to take me out long before Jerry did."

"I'll handle that shit. That's what the fuck we got people for. I'm gonna treat you the same way your ass treated Shaheem."

"Yeah, whatever," I chuckled.

"Kas I'm serious. I don't know about you, but that shooting changed the way I looked at life. I want out myself my nigga, but we built this shit too solid to let it fall. Julio is gonna have to bring another team in because I want out within eighteen months."

"I never thought I would hear that," I said.

"I never had an experience like losin' my brother. It's time for a nigga to settle down and make some babies of my own," he laughed.

"I feel you. You know you always got some businesses to fall back on. Make the moves you gotta make and do what you gotta do."

We pulled up to my crib and I dapped Jay up before climbing out and heading up to the house. I couldn't wait to step into my new life waiting on the other side of the door.

Chapter Twenty Four

Mercedes

"Cedes," I heard my name being called. I stopped bouncing Kash and froze in my spot. "Where you at, Ma?"

I quickly placed Kash in her bassinet before dashing towards the stairs. Standing at the front door was the love of my life. I couldn't stop the tears that welled in my eyes. I raced down the steps and damn near jumped in his arms.

"Shit, Mercedes! My chest man," he winced.

"I'm sorry," I said wiping my face. "I'm just so glad you're home. This has been the longest four weeks of my life. Not knowing if you were going to make it and trying to balance the three babies. This is like a dream come true."

"I know, Ma and I'm sorry. I'm here though. I'm gonna do all I can to help you. How are you feeling? Have you been resting?"

"Resting?" I scoffed. "What's that? I've been sore but sucking it up. I think I run on two hours of sleep a day. It's hard and I wonder how I do it."

"Superwoman," he smirked. "I'm here now. I'm outta the streets so my time is open. I want you to take care of yourself more too."

"Oh, look at you," I smirked. "You gotta take care of yourself too."

"I am. Trust me. I spent enough time away from y'all."

I wrapped my arms around Kas' neck and planted a kiss on his lips.

"Come on, let's go meet your girls officially," I said grabbing his hand and leading the way. He didn't hesitate to rush up the stairs behind me. All three of them were sleeping peacefully. Kas took his time walking around and taking in each one. Kassidy began stirring in her sleep and Kas wasted no time picking her up. Having her in his arms, I could see a different type of love he was experiencing. I immediately picked up my phone and started snapping photos. These were the moments I prayed for every day for the last twenty-three days, day in and day out. God finally answered my prayers and I couldn't be happier

*****

Three Months Later...

"Kaseem!" I yelled from the closet as I was pulling clothes off of the hanger. He appeared in the doorway holding Kassandra and Kashmere. "What are you doing? We're supposed to be packing."

"The babies needed me," he said. I rolled my eyes because he was always using the babies as an excuse.

"Go lay their sleeping asses down. If you don't pack, we won't be going no damn where," I snapped.

"Stop being so feisty. We still have two days before we leave."

"And we still have shit to do. Don't forget we still have to get everything situated for three babies."

"Mercedes, both my mother and your mother have children. They will be able to take care of them, they aren't dumb."

I shook my head and continued to pull my clothes off of the hanger. I wasn't about to argue with his ass. At this rate, he could go to the Bahamas in his damn boxers. I was over him. I dragged the suitcases out of the closet and opened them in the middle of the floor. I began going back and forth and packed my bags while Kas sat on the bed staring at the girls. Once I was done, I closed up my bag and pulled the bags down by the front door. I headed back up to the room, picked up Kassidy and sat on the bed.

"You're really not gonna pack my bag?"

"Nope. Didn't you just tell you to pack and you told me we still have two days? So, you have two days to pack your shit. When I was willing, you didn't wanna do it. Now I'm done, you got that." I propped up Kassidy and began breastfeeding her as Kas stared at me.

"Really?"

"*Really,*" I mimicked.

"A'ight, I'm gonna remember that."

"What did Smokey say? Remember it, write it down, I don't give a fuck," I repeated the movie before I busted out laughing.

"You got a lot of shit," he chuckled. "Can I tell you something?"

"Oh God. What did you do?" I asked.

"Why do I gotta do something?"

"What you gotta tell me, Kaseem?"

"Forget it. I was gonna give your punk ass a compliment, but I'll keep that shit to myself."

"Did you take your medication?" I asked, changing the

topic.

Kas sucked his teeth. "I don't need the medication Mercedes," he snapped.

"Your fuckin' attitude sucks! I'm just tryna help your ungrateful ass." I finished feeding Kassidy before burping her and putting her back in her bassinet. I was done talking to Kaseem. Over the last few months, I felt like I was nothing to him. Kas was an excellent father. He came home and jumped right into daddy mode, which I appreciated, but it's like he forgot we had a relationship. My feelings of neglect were at an all-time high.

I grabbed Kassandra from Kas and walked out, heading into the girls' room. I wanted to be alone. I knew my hormones had to still be out of whack but Kas' attitude towards me wasn't helping. I rocked slowly in the rocking chair as I breastfed Kassie. I closed my eyes and took a few deep breaths. I started praying again to God. I needed a sign that this would get better. I prayed so hard for Kas to come home and now that he was here, I felt like an outcast. By no means was I jealous of my daughter's. I loved that he was building a bond with them, but I just wanted him to remember I was here too.

I finished feeding Kassie, burped her and headed back to get Kash from Kas.

"Can we talk, Mercedes?"

"About?"

"Us."

My heart began racing. I placed Kassie in her bassinet and grabbed Kash to feed her.

"Okay, talk."

He sighed. "Look, I'm sorry. I know these last few months have been crazy. The girls keep our hands full. What I was tryna say to you earlier was thank you for all you do. Nobody would be able to that these are your first babies. You do this shit easily and make it look even easier."

Like I had been doing at the damn drop of a dime since I was pregnant, I began to cry.

"Why are you crying?" he asked as he leaned over to wipe my face.

"It's not easy Kas. I feel like I have a partner in parenting but that I'm single in this relationship. It's like you forget that we're supposed to be a unit."

"What? Why do you feel that way?"

"All of your attention is on the girls and when you're not tending to them, you're running out the door to tend to business, which I understand you have to do but in the midst of it all, I'm by myself. You hardly kiss me, let alone touch me. I can't even tell the last time we had sex," I cried. He scooped Kashmere out of my arms before laying her in her bassinet. He then grabbed me by my arms and pulled me up into his chest. I began sobbing heavily into his chest letting out all my stress, hurt, worries, and insecurities and Kas did what I needed him to do; hold me. Once I settled down, he looked me in my eyes again.

"Mercedes Castro, I would never forget or push you to the side. I try to be here for you and take the load off of you as much as I can. You always look so damn exhausted. Before I leave, I try and make sure the girls are settled before I do anything. I check on the businesses because that is our income. I check in with you to make sure you're good. I won't know what you need from me if you don't tell me. I would love to make love to you all fuckin' night, but when I watch you sleep; you look as though you need every single moment. Believe me, I would love to slide up in that and plant a few more seeds," he laughed. I mushed him and shook my head. "But Ma, I need you to remain open with me. I'm not a mind reader. If you have a need I'm not meeting, tell me so I can meet that need. You gotta communicate with me, babe. Now lovemaking is what you want?"

He ran his hands up and down my back. I closed my

eyes and enjoyed his touch. Kas began planting kisses all over my face and down my neck. I literally felt like I was melting in his hands. He softly pushed me backwards on to the bed. I felt like a timid teenager about to lose her virginity when he touched me. The love in his eyes is what I had been longing to see. His tender touches, I had been longing to feel.

He began lifting my shirt up and stopped. I was self-conscious of my C-section scar and immediately shot my hands over the spot. Kas looked at me crazy before moving my hands.

"Don't do that," he said. "You gave life. You brought three beautiful babies into this world through that spot right there. That is the most beautiful scar I've ever seen in my life." He kissed my scar softly before continuing to remove my clothes. He removed my pants and began nibbling on my clit through my panties. I lifted my ass off the bed trying to remove them before Kas popped my hand and continued nibbling. Before I could protest, he yanked so hard he immediately ripped them off.

"Wait, wait," I panted.

"Nah, this is what you wanted right? Let me do what I'm supposed to do. Sit back and enjoy this ride you've been missing," he said, and a ride is exactly what he took me on.

Chapter Twenty Five

Kaseem

I chuckled as I stared at Cedes who was passed out. One round and she was tapping out. As I thought about the way her legs shook, I shook my head and smirked before heading into the bathroom to take a quick shower. The girls were still sleeping from their nighttime feed.

Standing in the mirror, I stared at my scars and ran my hands across them. I still thanked God daily for bringing me out of the situation. Being around my girls made me want better. I had to admit, they couldn't have come at a more perfect time. I couldn't imagine having them while I was in the streets. The shit wouldn't have mixed well together.

Thankfully, I didn't have to worry about the street shit anymore. I could focus on the businesses, my lady and my kids.

*****

Two Days Later...

"Here's their bags with their clothes. I brought plenty of breast milk for them," Cedes told my mother.

"Girl get out," my mother said. "This isn't my first go-round with kids. If you waste my money and miss these damn flights, I'm gonna beat you like you're one of my damn kids."

I had to laugh because I know my mother meant every single word she said. My mother was one who didn't like to be told what to do regardless of who it was.

"I'm just trying to make sure you'll be fine," Cedes retorted.

"I'll be better when you get the hell out. Bye." She pushed us out the door. Cedes stood there with her mouth hung open. I chuckled and grabbed her hand, pulling her towards the car.

"Let's go. Let's go catch these flights." Sha was waiting in the car to drop us off. Once we got in the car and I could see Cedes' entire mood changing. "Come on Ma."

"I'm just gonna miss the girls," she sniffled.

"Ma, we have international calling. You can call them as much as you want but you have to enjoy yourself as well. You just told me you felt like we were losing ourselves in becoming parents. Let's use this time to find ourselves again. Let's get back to where we were," I told her.

She sighed, "You're right. I've just never been away from them for more than a few hours so to be away from them for days is nerve-wracking."

"You'll be fine, babe."

I squeezed her hand to assure her as we jumped on the highway heading towards the airport. Once Sha dropped us off, I grabbed our suitcases and headed inside to check-in. Surprisingly, TSA moved faster than I thought and Cedes, and I headed towards the gate.

Eight hours later, Cedes and I landed in sunny, beautiful Nassau, Bahamas. We grabbed our luggage and went out to the transportation vehicles. The heat in the Bahamas was a different type of heat than summers in Rhode Island. The amazement in Cedes' eyes was beautiful. I could tell she was falling in love with what she was seeing.

Pulling up to the resort, I had to admit the shit was dope. I was so wrapped up in looking around; I hadn't even seen the driver pull the bags out. He stood there and Cedes nudged me. I pulled out a twenty-dollar bill and handed it to the guy. We headed inside and checked in. They gave us bracelets for the drinks and gave us directions to the room. Before heading to the room, Cedes stopped at the bar and got her first drink. Cedes began squealing as we walked to the room.

"Babe, you gotta try this drink," she said passing me her cup. I took a quick sip and turned my face up. Cedes loved these fruity ass drinks made with cheap-ass liquor. Luckily, I had grabbed me a few bottles of Remy 1738 in the airport before getting in the van.

Unlocking the door, Cedes left her bag in the middle of the doorway.

"Oh my God! Do you see this view?"

I pulled her bag into the room and closed the door behind me. Cedes was sprinting through the room like a kid in a candy store.

"Kaseem, oh my God! If we ever get married, it has to be here. This shit is amazing!"

"Are you gonna sit down?" I asked her as I cracked the bottle on my Remy.

"I can't!"

"You can," I laughed. "Relax. We've been here five minutes and you're actin' crazy."

"No, I'm not," she plopped down on the bed. "But I'll

tell you what, this place may get you a fourth baby," she said winking.

"Don't threaten me with a good time. You'll go from a mom of three to six real quick," I warned.

"Nah, triplets won't happen again. My body better not betray me like that again. Releasing extra eggs and splitting shit. Nobody got time for that shit," she said finishing off her drink. "Matter fact, let me shower so I can take a nap and get ready to go fuck up this resort."

"You crazy as shit," I laughed. "Just a few hours ago, you were crying about leaving the babies and now your ass is ready to turn this island out."

"Fuck you, let me call my babies."

She dug her phone out and quickly called my mother.

"Mercedes don't make me add you to the blocked list," my mother answered.

"What? This is the first time I called."

"And it won't be the last. What do you need?"

"Can I see my babies?"

"Me too," I chimed in. My mother flipped the screen and showed all three of the girls sleeping in their car seats.

"Don't let them sleep in the chair overnight. It's not good for their back."

"Mercedes, how many kids do I have?" my mother

asked. "I know what I'm doing. How is the resort?" She turned the camera back towards her.

"Ma, this shit is dope," I answered. "You picked a nice ass spot. This view is killa!"

I took the phone from Cedes and showed my mother around the room as Cedes dug through her bag to get clothes. I chopped it up with my mother for a few more minutes before we hung up and I took another shot.

"Ma," I called out. "You wanna just kick it for the rest of the night?"

"I wanna go get something to eat and another drink," she said stepping out of the shower.

"A'ight. I'll jump in the shower real quick while you're getting dressed. Can you pull me out something?" I asked as I pulled my shirt over my head and kicked my sneakers off, followed by my shorts and boxers. I had to admit, this air conditioner felt fuckin' amazing. This Bahamian heat is no joke.

Within a half-hour, Cedes and I were hand in hand exploring the resort. It was a beautiful sight. We sat watching a group of kids playing with each other in the pool while the parents relaxed poolside with drinks. I definitely couldn't wait until the girls were older to enjoy trips like this. We went to a little dinner spot at the resort that was on the side of the pool. It had a nice open view of the pool and a swim-up bar. Cedes and I ordered food and another drink for her.

"This shit is really beautiful," Cedes said again.

"Did you mean what you said?" I asked her.

"About what?"

"Wanting to get married here."

"Please, you ain't gonna marry me," she brushed me off.

"What? You must be drunk or high or some shit. Why the hell would you think I wouldn't marry you?"

"You haven't asked yet and we've been together for four years."

I shook my head. Little did she know, I planned it Thanksgiving; that failed. I planned it for Christmas; that failed. I planned it for Valentine's Day; that failed. I dug in my pants pocket, pulled out the black velvet box and slid it across the table before standing.

"I got the receipt for that, so you can return it since '*I ain't gonna marry you*'." I walked away from the table leaving Cedes sitting by herself. I couldn't lie; I felt some type of way. My love for Cedes never wavered, regardless of what we went through. I knew from day one that Mercedes would be my wife. Every time I planned the perfect time, ironically, Mercedes always had a miscarried, which put a damper in the moment. When we found out she was pregnant with the twins and everything was going well, I planned the perfect timing for Thanksgiving. Due to my arrest, it threw a wrench in the plans. I wasn't expecting Cedes to stay upset with me as long as she did so both Christmas and Valentine's Day was a fluke too.

Me getting shot and missing the birth of my girls made me realize I needed to do this sooner rather than later. When she confirmed we were still taking the trip my moms got for us, I knew there wouldn't be a better place than on the beach in the Bahamas but now, it meant nothing. For once, I truly felt as though Cedes didn't know whether or not she really wanted to be with me. Maybe it was time for me to accept the fact that my lifestyle fucked up the best thing that happened to me. I guess it is what it is now.

Chapter Twenty Six

Mercedes

My heart broke and tears raced down my face as I called Kaseem's name, yet he continued to walk away from me. Picking up the box and opening it, I cried harder because the ring was everything I ever wanted. I remember like it was yesterday the day I was on Jared's website creating a ring I told Kas I wanted one day; he listened. Kaseem got the exact ring I designed, and it now hurt me deep that I said what I said.

I was a firm believer in a man knew right away whether he not he wanted to marry a woman. Kas would always make comments about me being his wife and saying he would marry me one day. When it didn't happen by the time that I had the girls, I just accepted he never would marry me.

Boy was I wrong.

And I felt like shit about it too.

I wanted to chase him but knowing Kaseem, he would ignore me. I threw my head in my hands and cried silently before picking up my phone. I scrolled through and tapped on Lex's name.

"Heyyyy, how is the Bahamas treating you?" she answered.

"Lex, I fucked up," I said just above a whisper.

"What? Bitch, you ain't been gone twelve hours. What the fuck you do?"

I ran down the conversation between Kas and I and I knew Lex was gonna let me have it.

"Them babies must've fucked your head up because ever since you've gotten pregnant, you've been one dumb ass broad. Do you remember that *you* stopped talking to *him*? Do you remember he chased your ass for months to get you back and you pushed him away? Now here y'all are getting shit back in order and you run your big ass mouth spitting out some nonsense. You're starting to act Janaya."

"Bitch don't ever insult me. We're not in the same

lane," I snapped.

"Call it what you wish. You might as well let the man go if you're not gonna let him love you right and you're not gonna love him right."

"Lex I would do anything for us to get back to where we were," I whined.

"It won't be that way Cedes. Y'all are parents now. Y'all are not the same adults you were seven months ago. Everyone changes and you gotta determine if that change fits you."

"I honestly can't see myself with anybody else," I told her honestly.

"Then act like it, Mercedes! In a minute, another bitch is gonna swoop right the fuck in and take what you claim you want." I didn't respond to what she said. "Listen, I know Kas hurt you Cedes when he hid his lifestyle. I get it, however, either forgive and move on or let him go and find love with someone else."

"There won't be someone else," I retorted.

"There will be before you even know it. Use this to find y'all again. Use this trip to determine if y'all are gonna be together or co-parent. But don't bring that bullshit back here around my babies. Go suck his dick and make up."

She hung up before I could say anything else. I sighed

before getting up and heading to the bar. I lost my appetite and just wanted one more drink before going to bed. As I waited for my drink, I decided to shoot Kas a text.

Me: (9:12pm) – Kaseem I love you; sometimes so much that I scare myself. We've been through so much and I know that we will conquer all that comes our way. I know I'm as stubborn as they come but I'm so glad you're able to deal with me. My fear is that one day, you'll no longer want me. Why do I feel that way? I have no idea because you've never even made me feel that way. I know you love me and, in my heart, I know this is where you want to be. I would like for us to find ourselves again while we're here, but I understand if you're done. I know my mood, attitude, and hormones have been a mess, but I hope you can find it in your heart to forgive me. I love you unconditionally.

I hit send, grabbed my drink and headed back to my room. I hoped Kas was there but if I knew him like I thought I did, he was gone somewhere clearing his head.

Opening the door, my assumption was correct. Kas was gone. I sighed deeply before stripping and climbing into the bed. I finished off my drink and allowed my thoughts to take me to sleep. I only prayed tomorrow would be better than today.

*****

Five days later, Kas and I were finally back home. We walked out of the airport and instantly spotted Lex waiting at the curb. The last five days in the Bahamas were absolutely fuckin' amazing! Kas and I made up and actually took the time to get to know each other again. We talked about everything under the sun and I personally felt as though we had become closer. I felt connected with Kas the same way I did before.

We had taken a lot of mini-trips together, but nothing topped the Bahamas. Between the resort and the excursions that we did on the island, I couldn't wait to go again, but I missed my girls like crazy.

"Hey Lex," Kas greeted. We hugged and put the luggage in the trunk.

"Hey, y'all! How was the trip?"

"Lex! OMG! You have to go, sis. It's gorgeous. We had such an amazing time."

"Really?"

"Yes! And thank you for the talk that night. I really needed it," I told her honestly.

"Good! Now Kas, did you officially pop the question?" she asked.

"Absolutely," I answered before Kas could. I flashed the ring in Lex's face.

"Oh shit! That's gorgeous. Good shit! You did real good Kas."

We pulled off from the airport towards Kas' mom's house. I fingered my ring as Kas and Lex rambled on about whatever they were talking about. I thought back to the night Kas officially popped the question.

We were walking along the beach behind the resort when he stopped randomly.

"Why did you stop?" I asked.

"Cedes," he sighed heavily.

"W-what? What's wrong?" My heart began racing and I just knew I had pushed him to the point where he was leaving me, and it was happening on this beach in the Bahamas.

"We've had some fucked-up times and some amazing times. We've had a lot of highs and minor lows. We've now welcomed three beautiful girls into this world, and I cannot thank you enough for them. I know it's not easy dealing with one, but you kill that shit with three. I promise you for as long as I live and beyond, you and my girls will not want for anything. While I'm here though, despite what you think, I want to spend the rest of my life with you. Will you marry a nigga?" he asked dropping to his knee.

My hands shot over my mouth in shock. I just knew he

would never pop the question after what I said, but here he was two days later, on his knee asking me to spend forever with him.

"Really?"

"Don't start this shit, Mercedes. I wouldn't be down here sinking in this sand for some fake shit. What's that line Usher says? If it's a question of my heart, you got it..."

"You're so corny!" I laughed. "Yes, of course, I'll spend forever and a fuckin' day with your ass."

I grabbed his hand and pulled him to his feet before kissing him deeply. Right there on the empty beach, Kas and I had some of the best sex I had ever had, sand in my ass and all. It was as if our connection and bond grew deeper.

"You gonna get outta the car or sit there and stare into space?" Kas asked. I realized then we were at his mother's house. I dashed out of the car and into the house to find my girls. Justine was sitting on the couch holding Kassidy and Kassandra while using her foot to rock Kashmere in her car seat. I scooped my baby out of her chair and smothered her in kisses.

"If you wake these girls," Justine threatened.

"Hush woman, I missed my babies and I'll wake them whenever I please," I joked. I handed Kashmere to Kas and grabbed the other two from Justine and did the same thing.

"I think they might be in the early stages of teething. Kash has been grunting while biting her hands like crazy," Justine said. "Kassandra and Kassidy have been drooling like hell. They weren't too cranky though."

"Thank God. They have those mitts at home with the rubber tips made for when they're teething, so I'll make sure to bust those out," I responded.

"What the hell is that?" Justine blurted as she grabbed my hand. "Y'all got married?"

"No," Kas chuckled. "I asked her to be my wife though."

"Aww, it's good to see y'all making it work.

I smiled at Kas as he was strapping Kash into her chair. I followed suit with the other two before saying our goodbyes and heading out to Kas' truck we left here. It's amazing what a week could change. I left here last week unsure about Kas and I and returned with a new understanding and engaged to the love of my life. I truly felt complete.

Epilogue

Kaseem
Nine Months Later...

"**M**ercedes, you ready?" I yelled as I put Kashmere's shoe on her foot. We were supposed to be gone an hour ago, yet Cedes was still taking her time.

"Yeah, I'm coming." She came downstairs and grabbed Baby Kass off of the floor. I grabbed Kash and Kassie and followed out behind her.

"I can't believe the girls are one," I said strapping them into their seats.

"How are you feeling?" she asked.

"What you mean?"

"It's the girls' birthday but it's also a year since you've been shot," she said.

"I won't remember this day for me damn near losing my life. I'll remember this day always as the day we went from a family of two to a family of five. I'm fine," I told her, and I meant it. I would be damned if I allowed a horrible event to overshadow the best day of my life.

"Glad you feel that way," Cedes said as we climbed into the car.

"How are you feeling?" I asked her.

"Stressed. I can't believe my babies are one! This has been one of the craziest years ever, but I wouldn't change it for the world."

"You ready for another one?" I asked.

"Don't try it," she laughed. "I would lose my mind with five kids."

"Five?"

"Nigga, your ass is just as much of a kid as the babies!"

"Fuck you," I joked.

"Aww babe, don't be mad at me," she said puckering up her lips for a kiss. I kissed her quickly before pulling away from the house. We were heading to the Fire Fighter's Hall where we were holding an *Uno* themed party for the girls. I know between Cedes, Lex and our mother's, this party was gonna be everything.

The moment we walked in, Kayla and my mother snatched the girls and began walking around with them showing them off. It was going to be a waste trying to get them back so Cedes entertained her people and I kicked it with Sha and Jay.

Jay was still on top of the game and I was proud of my nigga. I couldn't lie, I was missing the streets, but I couldn't go back. Even if I tried to, Jay wouldn't even let a nigga get down. Sha kept trying to hang into the street shit too, but Jay wasn't having that either. Me getting shot changed that nigga. His ass was even in the process of getting out and Julio was moving his youngest brother in to take over Jay's spot. Jay had a nigga keeping an eye on Shanie too. She thought because she moved out of state that she was in the clear, but she fucked with the wrong one. From what Jay told me, she became a boring ass bitch, which worked for me because I had a hot one for her and I didn't need to have her hanging with people who could be caught in a crossfire.

Jay and Cedes' sister Lex started kickin' it. Cedes was trying to intervene at first but I shut that down. We didn't like niggas in our shit, and I wasn't about to allow her to be in theirs. She respected it and as far as we knew, they were doing them. As long as one didn't do the other dirty, I had no issues.

I was standing by the door sipping on a Sprite when Cedes came and wrapped her arms around my waist.

"Are you okay?"

"Yeah, Ma. I'm good. Just thinking about how far I've come, the shit we've been through and the things we have yet to go through," I told her.

"Regardless of it all, just know that I'm here until the very end. I have something to tell you though," she said.

"What's up?" I asked pulling her to the front of me and resting my arms on her shoulders.

"We're expanding."

"Huh?"

"I'm pregnant."

"What?"

"With twins."

"Get the fuck outta here! Are you serious?"

She smiled and let a tear roll down her face.

"I have no idea how the fuck I'm gonna do it with five kids under two, but it is what it is now," she said.

"Regardless of whether it's three, five, seven, or ten, I'll be here alongside you raising all of them. I'm glad we're doing this shit together though."

"One thing though," she said. "We got to hold off on the wedding because I gotta drop these loads and drop this back to back baby weight. Five kids in two years, I gotta be one crazy-ass bitch with some loose ass eggs," she laughed.

"You got that, Ma. If you wanted to wait another five years, I would. Whenever you're ready, we'll do this," I told her before kissing her forehead. "We're in this for life."

"I love you."

"I love you more."

Cedes took me by surprise with her pregnancy announcement, especially saying she was having twins, but I meant what I said; I wouldn't want to be going through this thing called life with anybody else. I had no idea what God's plans were for me, but I knew one thing was for certain; I was ready to ride this ride with my family in the front row. I went from Kas the street nigga to Kas the businessman, father, and future husband. Cedes and my girls were all I needed in life and I wouldn't do shit else ever to jeopardize that.

The End

About The Author

Leondra LeRae grew up in Providence, RI. She is the mother of a little girl who is her pride and joy. She has dreams of becoming an OBGYN but enjoys writing in her free time. At 19, she self-published her first urban fiction novel

At 20 years old, Leondra signed to SBR Publications where she released National Best Seller; Official Street Queen.

Feel free to interact with her
Like her fan page:
www.facebook.com/AuthorLeondraLeRae
Follow her on Twitter: www.twitter.com/LeondraLeRae
Instagram: www.instragram.com/leo_xo
Email: authorleondralerae@gmail.com

Select Any Other of Her Reads on Amazon at:
www.amazon.com/author/leondralerae

$$\begin{array}{r} 220 \\ 100 \\ \hline 320 \end{array}$$

$$\begin{array}{r} 500 \\ 320 \\ \hline 180 \end{array}$$

Made in the USA
Monee, IL
04 September 2020